Death in the 12th House

Books by Mitchell Scott Lewis

Murder in the 11th House
Death in the 12th House

Death in the 12th House

Where Neptune Rules

A Starlight Detective Agency Mystery

Mitchell Scott Lewis

Poisoned Pen Press

Poisoned
Pen
Press

Copyright © 2012 by Mitchell Scott Lewis

First Edition 2012

10 9 8 7 6 5 4 3 2 1

Library of Congress Catalog Card Number: 2012910473

ISBN: 9781464200588   Hardcover
       9781464200601   Trade Paperback

Poisoned Pen Press
6962 E. First Ave., Ste. 103
Scottsdale, AZ 85251
www.poisonedpenpress.com
info@poisonedpenpress.com

Printed in the United States of America

For music and astrology
The two great loves of my life
Forever in harmony

And for Goldie
Constant in an ever changing universe

Acknowledgments

To my agent Sandra Bond, with sincere gratitude for all your help and guidance.

To Jessica Tribble, Annette Rogers, Robert Rosenwald, Barbara Peters, and all the wonderful people at Poisoned Pen Press: for your endless aid and support. And to Maryglenn McCombs for your so-appreciated tireless efforts and optimism.

To Fiona Druckenmiller and Roberta Cary, for your unwavering friendship, faith, and stability.

To my dear friends and family who have helped in so many ways: Ray Blumenfeld, Natalie Cagle, Anna Cody, Margaret Dorn, my mother Sidney Lewis, and my bother David Lewis.

And to my brilliant editor and friend Carl Lennertz, whose constant clarity and wisdom continue to amaze me. Two down and many more to go!

Grapes plucked from a nearly vacant vine
Quench better than the sweetest wine
—Marty Winebeck

Prologue

Freddie Finger was used to being stared at.

As the front man and lead singer for the band Rocket Fire, he had played to stadium-sized audiences. Their records had sold sixty million copies and the royalties had made Freddie a rich man. Despite his oversized ears and cow-like eyes, hardly a woman alive seemed to be able to resist him.

Freddie had bedded hundreds of women in his sixty-three years on the planet. The first when he was just fourteen, after his mother's friend saw him poolside at the Riviera Beach Club in New Rochelle. Their affair lasted about six months until Freddie's mother found out and threatened to call the police. But it didn't prevent Freddie with his now-awakened sexuality from finding other willing playmates.

During the hey-day of rock 'n roll in the seventies and eighties Freddie and the boys toured America, Europe, and Japan, and topped the charts with such libidinous titles as: "Red Panties," "Escalator to my Bed," and their biggest hit, "Cream on Me." They partied themselves into the record books with rivers of booze and mountains of cocaine. Females of all ages threw themselves at the band. The five had been friends since they were teenagers and felt more like brothers, sometimes fighting with each other but always protecting the clan against a demanding, hostile outside world.

But by the beginning of the Clinton administration the booze and drugs had taken their toll. They fought all the time. Their records, when they could work through the disagreements long enough to get one made, went nowhere, and they were forced to cancel a tour when Freddie was found unconscious in his hotel room, the result of a three-day binge. Their record company dropped them. Nobody else was willing to sign up a drugged-out has-been rock group from the dinosaur era.

After all seemed lost, a contract was offered to Rocket Fire by Dirk Warren, president of Nimble Records, under the stipulation that everyone in the band go into drug rehab and group therapy. In the past these bad boys of rock would have scoffed at the idea, but they knew this was their last chance. The boys agreed to the offer and entered Walnut Hill rehab in Oregon.

Eighteen months later they were stone cold clean and had the number one album and single in America. They put out three more hit albums, charting seven top 20s.

Even though he was sober and had no intention of ever slipping again, Freddie still liked to hang out in bars, especially in New York City.

He walked into Cantaloupe's Restaurant on Third Avenue and hiked his lean, aging frame up onto a stool at the ancient oak bar. The place had been there for decades. Freddie used to come in for burgers and beer. The jukebox fit the place and the music never changed. It was playing one seventies oldie after another.

A gray-haired man nudged his date. She looked up and they whispered something to each other. A few other patrons glanced Freddie's way. In New York it's considered chic to notice and then ignore celebrities.

Freddie ordered a cranberry and club. The bartender, a middle-aged buxom blonde with an infectious smile, placed it on a bev nap in front of him.

"How are ya, Freddie?" she asked, in a most familiar way.

He was used to that. People thought they knew you personally if you were famous.

"Fine, you?"

"You don't remember me, do you?"

Freddie searched his memory. Nothing. For about three decades he had been either drunk or hung-over and didn't remember many people.

She let out a big booming laugh. "That's all right, I don't look exactly like I used to."

"Who does?"

But there was something familiar about the laugh that was beginning to register. She saw the glimmer of recognition in his eyes. "Starting to come back to you, dearie?"

"Kitty?"

She smiled broadly. Then she leaned over the bar and planted a firm open-mouthed kiss on his lips for several moments, while the patrons looked on in awe.

His mind raced back. Way, way back. Back to when it all began, the summer of '69. They were a fledgling band of kids then, mostly doing covers of old blues songs and just learning how to write their own. It would be five years before they put out their first record. He had gone to Woodstock with some high school friends. They camped by the hill, which became known as Mud Village by the second rain-soaked day. That was where he met Kitty. For two days they made love in the rain. Then they said goodbye. Years later when Rocket Fire landed on the charts, Kitty found Freddie backstage after a show in Boston. They rekindled their passion several times in those heady days and then lost touch once again.

Until tonight.

New York cool be damned. People began to come up to him, some shaking his hand, a few just looking on. He signed a few autographs and posed next to fans for two phone camera pictures.

Suddenly Freddie was overcome with a wave of nausea. He got up and held on to the bar for support. His mouth felt dry and a thin cloud began to veil his sight. He put down a hundred, pushed through the throng, and walked toward the door.

His vision grew blurred. "Shit," he said out loud.

He stumbled out the door, walked halfway down the street, and sat on a building stoop trying to clear his head. The streets were very quiet. It was Thursday night before the Fourth of July holiday weekend and every New Yorker who could afford it was already out of the city.

He heard footsteps on the deserted street. Someone stopped a few feet from him. He looked up, shook his head trying to focus. He squinted into the face.

"You?" he asked. "What the hell are you doing here?"

"Shh," an index finger on the lips.

Freddie tried to stand but couldn't get his legs to respond. He looked up, tried to say something, and then passed out.

Freddie was always skinny. He weighed about one fifty after a big meal. It wasn't difficult to haul his flaccid body over to a blue car. He was tossed into the backseat.

He had always loved cars, had a garage full of exotic and expensive automobiles from many different eras. He said that driving was the one place you could really be alone and free in this world.

This was the last ride Freddie would ever take.

Chapter One

David Lowell was walking down Second Avenue when the rain began. It was a little before six in the morning and promised to be a hot July day. Dressed in his usual garb of loafers, blue jeans pressed to a firm crease, and light-weight cotton turtleneck, he was strolling from his townhouse on East 93rd Street to his office on 24th as was his custom, no matter what the weather. The rain was warm. He opened his umbrella and continued to amble through the mostly empty streets.

This was the only part of the day he could call his own. No phone calls or obligations, no hysterical clients or problems to be solved. They could all wait a few hours. This was his time.

Second Avenue wasn't the same boulevard he had grown to know over the decades. Construction for the ill-conceived new subway line had destroyed much life along this once thriving thoroughfare, forcing dozens of small businesses to close. Deep underground, the tunneling was creating a disaster for the Upper Eastside here on the surface. As he walked past a dogwood tree planted in one of the few tiny square spaces allotted for nature on this urban island, he saw a rat the size of a small dog scurry into a hole next to the tree. He shook his head at what this previously pristine district had become.

He passed Tony's DeNapoli, a neighborhood fixture for decades, closed now, another victim of the subway and the expansionist philosophy that was pervasive throughout New York City. One empty storefront followed another, some with for-rent signs, others not even bothering until construction was completed. And all for a thirty block rail running under the affluent east side. *The rich man's subway*, he'd heard it called a number of times. Or *Bloomberg's Trolley*. It was the landlord's delight. Soon they'd be able to advertise apartments along the river as "two blocks from the subway," and charge twice the rent.

He liked the rain, even on a warm July morning. It gave him an atmosphere conducive to deep thought. His daughter would say it was depression. And he liked walking the Manhattan streets, especially when they were relatively vacant. He had begun taking these long morning walks when he'd first opened his detective business seven years ago and found that they cleared his mind and prepared him for the day's tasks better than anything.

He turned down 24th Street just as the rain let up, stopped into a deli for coffee and a muffin, and went into his office building. He took the elevator to the sixth floor and entered the suite of offices. It was empty. And quiet. He turned on the lamp in the reception area, then opened the door to his inner office and went in.

The leather couch was a pull-out with a king size, orthopedic mattress. The detective's private bathroom contained a full-sized tub and shower and a completely modern kitchen hid behind one of the doors. Lowell would often spend several days and nights in the room when working on a case.

He switched on the ceiling fan and stood gazing out the window in admiration at his unobstructed view of the Empire State Building. A big glass tank stood next to the window, containing water, rocks, and two rather large turtles.

"Hello, Buster." He lightly touched one of the turtles on the head. The other slowly walked the two steps to where his finger was moving and pushed its head up. Lowell obliged with a gentle scratch. "Hello, Keaton." He sprinkled some food into the tank and watched them eat breakfast. Satisfied, the two turtles moved laboriously toward the water in the middle of the tank and tucked their heads into their shells. Lowell often envied that ability.

◇◇◇

A little before nine Sarah came to the front door of the Starlight Detective Agency office, one hand laden with packages, a large cup of deli coffee in the other. An umbrella hung on her wrist dripping a small puddle at her feet. She struggled to remove her keys from her purse without setting down all of her belongings. After almost spilling the coffee several times, she gave up and put her things on the ground, took out her key and opened the door. She pushed her bright red hair back behind her ears, picked everything up, and entered.

Sarah set the coffee down on her desk, hung up her hat and umbrella, and sat down, immediately checking the answering machine. She scribbled down all the relevant information, drank about half of her coffee, and settled in for another day as astrologer-detective David Lowell's assistant. When she saw the lamp on her desk had been turned on she knew Lowell was in his office. She hit the intercom and buzzed twice, their code to let him know she had arrived. Ten minutes later the intercom buzzed back.

"Yes, boss?"

"Any important messages?"

"Just the usual. A few clients, two reporters seeking interviews. Melinda called."

"Okay, get her on the phone. The rest can wait."

A few moments later his phone rang.

"Hi, dad."

"You called?"

"Just wanted you to know I'm going to Dallas on a case for a few days."

"Anything exciting?"

"Not really, just a malpractice suit."

"That law firm is running you ragged."

"That's what you get when you're the junior associate. I'll be fine, really."

"Well, be careful and keep in touch."

"I'll text you every day."

He snorted. "Text. Why can't you call me?'

"Okay, dad, I'll call. But you know…"

"If you tell me one more time that the world has changed and I have to keep up with it, I'll throttle myself. Besides, I now use an iPad, so you can't say I'm not changing. I'd just rather hear your voice than read six words in a text."

She laughed. "Okay, I'll call you, I promise."

◇◇◇

About eleven Lowell's intercom buzzed.

"Lieutenant Roland is here. He'd like to see you." She whispered, "He doesn't look happy."

"Send him in."

The door opened and one of NYPD's finest entered.

"Hey, Lieutenant, what brings you around?" Lowell unconsciously pulled the band off his ponytail, straightened the long, graying hair, and retied it.

The policeman sat in a leather chair.

"Well, I'm getting serious pressure to bring you in on a case."

Lowell leaned back in his plain meshed-back chair. He had tried every fancy ergonomic chair, figuring if he was going to spend a third of his life in it, it should be the best. None felt right, until he found that the simplest model on sale at Staples suited him just fine. "That's rather unusual. I didn't think the police department liked to hire outside detectives."

"Well, this is an unusual case. And we wouldn't be hiring you directly."

"Tell me about it?"

"There's been another." Roland's raised eyebrows said it all.

Lowell rested his chin on his fingertips. "You mean another rock 'n roll killing?"

"Yep. This is the third. First Gene Hallow, then Wally Fischer. Two is a coincidence. Three is a trend."

"Who is the most recent victim?"

"You know Freddie Finger?"

"From Rocket Fire? Hell, I saw them once." Lowell went quiet, thinking back to all the concerts he and his ex-wife had gone to.

"Lowell?"

"Sorry, I'm back. How did it happen?"

"The body was found in a building undergoing renovation on 80th between First and Second. A five-floor townhouse in the last stages of work, recently put on the market. Some workmen came in this morning to clean up and found him on the second floor hanging from a heat pipe. The ME says he was killed last night, probably around midnight. He was shot three times first, and then strung up. The shooting went down somewhere else. No blood at the apartment."

"Christ."

They were both silent for a moment.

Roland looked at his notes. "A pack of matches was found in his pocket from a neighborhood restaurant called Cantaloupe's. The bartender remembers him being there and leaving alone. She also remembers an odd man with a heavy accent, she thought maybe German, leaving shortly after."

"So who's pressuring you to bring me in?"

"It's his daughter. She lives in LA, but is here visiting and called me as soon as she heard. She asked if I would make the introductions and get you on board. Apparently your Winston case got a lot of publicity on the West Coast too, and she pretty much demanded that I include you in the investigation."

"There's no reason I have to be actively involved. Why don't you just consult me and I can do my work from here."

"I can think of two reasons right off the bat. First of all, she's a very influential person, and if she finds out you aren't actively working on this case she can make my life miserable…"

"…and the second reason is that every minute she's annoying me is one less she's on your back."

"Absolutely." Roland smiled.

Lowell held up his hand. "Who is this celebrated client we are about to share?"

"Vivian Younger." The Lieutenant said it with a touch of drama.

"Vivian Younger, the actress?"

"Actress, model, singer…you name it, she's into it. Didn't you know she was Freddie's daughter? Now do you see the spot I'm in?"

Lowell sat back in his chair and tugged on his ponytail, his thoughtful tic. "Hmm, yes I see your difficulty. I assume this will hit the papers today."

"No way to keep it out. The guy was an icon, for god's sake. I'm getting pressure from everybody, Freddie's record company, his manager, promoters. And now I'm getting even more from Vivian Younger's press secretary, her attorney, even the mayor's office."

"They all must have been about sixty, wouldn't you say? The murder of three aging rockers." Lowell leaned back in the chair with his hands clasped behind his head. "All right then, I'll take the case."

"Good. I'll introduce you to her later today." The Lieutenant extended his hand. "Thank you, Lowell, I appreciate it. And one more thing."

"I know, don't talk to the press."

"Actually, in this case you won't have a choice. As if Freddie weren't enough, Vivian Younger is such hot news that you can't avoid them."

Lowell groaned audibly.

"Just be careful what you say."

"In case you've forgotten, I don't care too much for the press, or the public."

"There's a patrol car waiting downstairs to take you to the murder scene when you're ready."

"That's okay. I'll use my car and driver."

"Fine." Roland handed Lowell a manila folder. "Here is the address of the townhouse and the birth information of the three victims. I'll meet you there in an hour."

Before the lieutenant was out of his chair, Lowell had swiveled to his computer and started typing. He punched in the three victims' information and printed out the charts. Then he grabbed his iPad, had Sarah call his driver, Andy, and headed out the door.

Chapter Two

The townhouse had been gutted and its contents piled in an ugly trash container on the street that took up two precious parking spots. New windows and a door had already been installed and it appeared that only cosmetic improvements remained to be done. Outside several policemen kept the public at bay behind the crime scene tape. The story had headlined the morning news shows and several had mentioned the address where Freddie was found. As Lowell got out of his car, heads turned to see who it was. The crime-scene gawkers were clad in all manner of clothing, from ties to overalls, baseball caps to a guy wearing a hooded sweatshirt, even on such a warm day. Lowell heard the click of a few cellphone cameras.

The rain stopped. He walked into the townhouse and was met by another officer who recognized the astrologer.

"Hey, professor. Am I glad I ran into you. You remember the last time I saw you, you were kind enough to take a look at my wife's chart?"

"Of course. Officer…" Lowell looked at the cop's shirt. "… Browning, how nice to see you again. How is she doing?"

"She's just fine, thanks to you. You were absolutely right about the medicine affecting her liver. The doctors said if she'd been kept on it even another month it might have been fatal. Thank God you said something."

"I merely noticed a Jupiter-Neptune affliction in the natal chart being transited by Pluto that set off a warning bell and I thought you should address it. I'm happy it turned out okay."

"Yes sir, if there's anything you need just ask me. You here officially, or what?"

Lowell laughed. "Yes, officer, this time everything's on the up and up."

"Well, you have any problems, you let me know. And it's Billy, by the way."

"All right, Billy, thank you. Where was the body found?"

"The room right at the top of the stairs, you can't miss it. Hey, Franks," he called up the stairs, "he's all right to come up."

Lowell climbed the winding staircase. He entered the unfurnished room, now brightly lit from three windows with a southeastern view. Most New Yorkers thought Manhattan ran perfectly north-south, like a compass, but in fact, it was askew, as this view proved.

The body had been removed earlier, but the rope was still hanging from the heat pipe in the ceiling. Lowell walked around the room taking in as much as he could. The officer stood by the front door.

"What do you think this place goes for?"

The officer scratched his head and looked around. "More than I got."

"Five floors, a view like this and, if I'm not mistaken, an enclosed backyard. In this market – Christ, must be about ten million. So how come he chose to bring Freddie here? I don't think that was accidental, nor a matter of convenience."

Lowell and the officer turned toward the hallway at the sound of footfalls on the uncarpeted steps.

Roland entered. "Ah, glad you're here, Lowell. This is Vivian Younger, Freddie's daughter."

That she was a Gemini was apparent at first glance to the astrologer's trained eye: tall, slim, a long thin neck and broad shoulders, pale hair, a high forehead, piercing eyes and sharp features. She had that Gemini ability to appear different from each angle. On first view she seemed young, almost waiflike, and painfully fragile, her face, like a china cup, too delicate to handle. Yet if she turned a bit to the left or the right, the light reflected an entirely different persona: bold and strong, a bit arrogant and incredibly womanly. She wasn't beautiful in the traditional sense of the word, but her face was so animated it was impossible not to stare at her.

"David Lowell." He extended his hand.

Hers was warm and soft, but the shake was firm and directed. A tear trickled down her left cheek. She managed a smile, wiping away the droplet with a finger. "Thank you for being here, Mr. Lowell."

"David, please."

"Ms. Younger insisted on seeing the, uh, place where, uh that is…" fumbled the lieutenant.

"I understand," said Lowell. "Sometimes we must have closure at any cost."

"What do you make of this location?" asked the lieutenant.

"Ms. Younger, do you mind if I speak bluntly? I don't mean to be insensitive."

"No, please. I want to hear what you think."

"Well, I'm sure your father's was not a random killing. There was much forethought put into the planning of this crime. By the way, I believe he was killed a bit after midnight, probably about 12:15 or so, after the Moon entered Virgo. Before that time the moon was Void of Course and there were probably several mistakes made that could have delayed or ruined the murderer's plans. However, like I said this was a well planned attack. Transiting Mercury opposed your father's natal Pluto, indicating a potentially underhanded or hidden agenda being acted out. Mars, the god of war, and ruler of the ego, was conjunct his natal Neptune, ruler of drugs. You will probably find traces of a knockout drug in his system. What about alcohol?"

"No, my father had been sober for years. You won't find any alcohol in his system unless it was forced upon him."

"You don't believe he could have fallen off the wagon?"

She shook her head. "If you knew what he went through to get sober you'd never ask that question. My father loved music more than anything in the world. Drinking almost cost him his career. He wasn't going to risk losing it again."

"I've seen what I need to here, Ms. Younger. Why don't we get some tea?"

"Call me Vivian, and yes, tea would be nice."

"Lieutenant, I'll call you later at the precinct."

The crowd had thinned out by now. Among the few left was the guy in the hooded sweatshirt, who looked down as if to hide his face, Lowell noticed, the second Lowell passed with Vivian.

They made it to the corner, crossed the avenue, and as they walked in silence down the street, Lowell and Vivian approached a man maybe fifty, dressed in jeans and an NYU sweatshirt, ostensibly vacuuming the sidewalk with a Hoover upright, although there was no electric chord visible, and it made no sound. The man had put together a make-shift room, complete with a black leather chair, torn across the seat, next to a table holding a lamp, which was also unplugged. There was even a magazine rack on the ground next to the chair with several old issues of *Time* in evidence. Apparently someone had emptied out an apartment, and this gentleman had commandeered a tiny piece of the city as his own.

"Don't stop, don't stop," he said, as they walked past. "Nothing left, it's all taken. And there's no room, no room." Defiantly he sat in his armchair and grabbed a copy of *Time*, opening it with great panache and holding it up to his face.

Lowell was forced to smile at the glory of a man, deranged as he was, struggling against the tides of his life. There was something gallant about his unwillingness to give up. He had found refuge and a temporary home on the street and he had claimed it.

There wasn't a hat or a cup out for money, but they couldn't pass without offering some help. It wasn't the time or place to debate if giving money like this only postponed the inevitable, or if a donation just assuaged the giver's guilt. Vivian reached in her purse, fished around, and handed Lowell a twenty dollar bill. He added one of his own, and he tucked both under the base of the lamp.

The man kept the magazine glued to the front of his face.

Chapter Three

Lowell and Vivian arrived at a tiny bistro sandwiched between a Thai place and a Middle Eastern restaurant, where they were seated immediately. Vivian slid into the leather booth against the wall, and Lowell took the chair. She was dressed in a yellow blouse, a pastel blue skirt, and yellow shoes. A single strand of pearls adorned her neck, and two rings, one on each pinkie, completed her ensemble. There was a simplicity about her that Lowell appreciated.

When they were seated, they ordered two teas. Vivian asked for honey for hers. She began right away.

"I read about you in the LA papers. They said you're some sort of genius, and that you have helped the police solve crimes in the past, although how an astrologer can do that I really don't know." She blew out a breath. "But if you can help find my father's killers I would be eternally grateful."

Her uncertainty about his profession was not something new to Lowell. How often in his life had people scoffed at his calling, all the way back to the seventies in Cambridge, Massachusetts, when he first began his studies.

"You can't tell someone's fortune from their birthday," he could hear his friends beseeching him. The very same friends who, through the years, would eventually come to him seeking help, most having long ago become converts. He had foreseen divorces, accidents, and diseases long before they manifested.

He had told his friends things about their young children that, as time went by, had come to pass.

"Tell me what you think astrology is?" Lowell threw the question out as nicely as possible.

"Well, mostly what I read in the newspapers and magazines. I like the woman who writes for *New Fashion*, she's pretty good. But it's all very general, isn't it?"

He shook his head. "That's not astrology. That's American newspaper sun-sign astrology, more for entertainment than real knowledge. Although some are really written by excellent professional astrologers, many of those articles aren't even written by real astrologers at all, but by writers who either use a known astrologer for a front, or make up a name altogether. If you want to read about real astrology, pick up *Dell Horoscope Magazine*, or *The Mountain Astrologer*, and you can see what some of the best people working in the field have to say. Astrology is a very personal business, and it's difficult to write something meaningful that will suit all Capricorns or Libras. I tell you what, you write a column for me, right now. Let's say I need one for Monday for the sign of Cancer. What do you know about the Crab?"

She looked thoughtful. "Okay. They're supposed to be very sensitive, sometimes too much so, I'm told. They like to stay at home and they can sometimes lose their temper easily when emotional. Oh, I see. So it's Monday, well…Cancer: Be careful today, you may be a bit touchy, um…especially in the morning. Plan to spend the evening with friends or a loved one. You will be…more receptive and it will help balance the day, something Cancers always like."

He smiled. "You're hired. Put my name on the byline and we'll get syndicated in a hundred newspapers across the U.S. We'll make a bundle just on that."

"Wow, and it's all faked?"

"Not one bit of astrology is fake." He smiled as the waitress put two cups, saucers, and small metal hot water pots in front of them. Vivian ripped open her tea bag cover and poured the hot water over the bag into her cup. Lowell opened the paper tea cover slowly, and holding the string between his fingers, dipped the bag into the metal pot. The process let him gather his thoughts. "Let me make that completely clear. It's just been watered down through pop culture. Astrology is an intricate, mathematically precise science we now call astronomy, coupled with an intuitive art that connects a humanist response to the celestial events. This connection between intellect and intuition is something that seems difficult for western man, especially Americans, to recognize."

"Why is that?"

"For one thing, people don't like the concept of things being taken out of their control. Many seem to feel astrology does that."

"Doesn't it?"

"Just the opposite. It allows us to use the energies of the universe around us to our advantage. The stars do not force our actions, they only show us what resistance we may be facing and creative ways around it. And if you want to talk about having control taken away from you, what do you think God and religion does? It not only takes away control but culpability as well. And by the way, formal religion, which now publicly denounces astrology, embraced it in its early years. Perhaps the powers that be felt it was too God-like, maybe too much power in the hands of a few humans who could interpret what was going on. They felt it was blasphemous."

"What do you think?"

"I think that God, if he or she does exist, is probably quite aware of what we call astrology. I doubt that God woke up one day and said: "Damn, those little monkeys, they discovered my secret about the stars. How can I keep them from learning how to use it and from finding out other stuff? I know, I'll have them invent money, that'll keep them busy, and teach them a lesson at the same time.""

She laughed. He liked her laugh, but of course, so did millions of fans. She didn't seem much like a movie star at all. More like the prettiest girl in class you were never able to get up the courage to talk to.

"There is a great deal a good astrologer can know about a person."

"What can you tell about me?"

"I don't know, let's see." He opened the cover of his iPad and put it on the table. "I'll need your birth information. And no cheating." He smiled.

"June 13th at 6:32 a.m. in New Rochelle, New York."

"Uh huh, and the year?"

"Do I have to?" She smiled.

"Sort of defeats the whole purpose of planetary positioning if I don't know the year."

She sighed. "Well, if I must." She leaned over the table and whispered into his ear, "1978."

He cleared his throat and typed the information into the device, then sat back, his expression becoming more business-like as he viewed the birth chart.

"Well, this certainly is the chart of a person with a prominent relationship to the public, although in a few years you will most likely withdraw from performing. You might then work behind the scenes, perhaps as a director or writer. You have a Cancer rising sign, which makes you very attractive and feminine. Jupiter and Venus in the first house show the kind of relationship you have with the public, quite simply they adore you. The Sun rules your 2nd house of money, and the Virgo Moon squares it, which tells me that you must learn to handle your resources better, as any emotional instability will throw off your common sense, causing you to spend frivolously. The Sun represents what you want in life, and the Moon indicates what you need. When these two are in square, it implies that what you want and what you need can be in conflict. And because of the frustration that this can produce, you can be your own worst enemy, and at times make very bad decisions. It indicates your parents were probably divorced, and with the Moon in the 4th house you lived with your mother. Your Sun is afflicted in the 12th house, which shows that your father may have had a drug or alcohol problem, and could have been in some sort of institution, either prison or hospitals, while you were quite young. With the 12th house Sun in Gemini also ruling the 3rd house of siblings you might have had a brother or sister, possibly even a twin who was lost, perhaps through an early death. The 12th house Mercury opposes a retrograde Neptune in the 6th house of health, which shows that you may have a weakness in your lungs, possibly caused by an infection, that must be carefully monitored and you should never smoke. How'm I doing?" Lowell tugged at his ponytail, and patiently awaited her response.

She was sitting quite still with her elbows resting on the table. She had not moved as Lowell talked. Finally she slowly shook her head.

"Nobody knows that I had a twin who died at birth. Nobody. Only my family. My parents *were* divorced, but you could learn that anywhere. My father spent several stints in rehab, but again, common knowledge. I have also been diagnosed with a recurring pulmonary disease as a result of an infection and fever I had as a child, presently in remission. But none of this information made the papers, my press agent made sure of that. How could you know? I have been losing my desire to be in the public eye for some time now, and have considered trying my hand at directing. But I've spoken to no one about this."

He nodded.

"How," she stopped, and then began again. "How do you think I'll do?"

"Quite well. You should be very successful in your second career, although the public will not let you go easily. You project something optimistic and airy that the collective needs. You will occasionally come out of retirement as a performer throughout the years."

There was something about this man that made her feel calmer, more secure. His knowledge was comforting. He certainly wasn't her type. He was too short and much too old. Still, she felt safe in his presence.

"So how did you become…"

"An astrologer?"

"Actually I was going to say a detective. I assume the astrology came at a young impressionable age when you were looking for answers."

"That's quite accurate."

"And as you realized its capabilities you must have been drawn into it from curiosity as well as a desire for self-awareness. How'm I doin'?"

He smiled. "Not bad."

"So how about it? What made you become an astrological detective instead of just staying a professional astrologer?"

"I've been doing astrology for more than thirty years, and during that time I have had to help many people make the most important decisions of their lives. Financial ones, health ones. I've diagnosed cancer and thyroid problems, kidney stones, heart murmurs, and infections hidden from view in clients, some of whom were thousands of miles away. People needed to know what day to have an operation or when to start a business. I felt that I could never be wrong, and no matter how hard I worked there was never enough time to see the number of clients required to make a good living. Well, after a while the stress was becoming too much, but by then I had a family and I needed the money. So I shifted my focus."

He poured more tea into his cup.

"I'm giving a lecture at the Ivy League Club next week on political and financial astrology. If you're still in town why don't you come?"

"I'd love to."

"My audience is usually a good mixture of Wall Street executives, artists, and occasionally a politician or two. I usually discuss the financial and political future of America and the world. And yes," he said, answering her unasked question, "they do believe in astrology, even the skeptics, after having seen what it can do for many years. Although I wonder how many would admit it in public.

"Anyway, in the early nineties I went to the New York Mercantile Exchange and began studying the financial markets, using astrology to trade. It worked so well that I built a reputation as an astro-economist, working for several large firms and making predictions in commodities, stocks, and bonds. I managed to build up enough capital to take advantage of Pluto, the ruler of oil, entering Sagittarius, the most expansive of signs. I convinced a wealthy client to buy oil options and futures when it was trading about $30 a barrel and rode the market as the price went to $140, making a very nice profit."

That, of course, was part of the answer. And it was true, as far as it went. After decades of private practice he had started to become overwhelmed, and had been seriously considering a change of professions, though never of avocation. The only obstacle was finances. But the oil trade took care of that problem. So sure was he that oil prices were about to explode that he had invested everything he had, plus what he could borrow, to invest. It had made him a very wealthy man.

But this wasn't something he readily shared with others. People responded strangely to huge amounts of money, even rich or famous people, sometimes in a destructive or uncomfortable way.

She stared at him with fascination. She had always thought of astrology as a party gimmick or a carnival game. "But you still haven't told me why you became a detective."

"No, I haven't. Something…happened several years ago that required that I pay attention to the criminal element in our culture, and I guess it became a habit." His hands, which had been helping him narrate his tale, dropped to the table.

She didn't press it.

When they were finished he called his driver and took her back to her hotel. In the past she had always stayed at the Plaza, but the icon had been mostly turned into another palace of condos and corporate apartments. Now she stayed at the Carlyle on upper Madison Avenue.

She reached for the car door handle but stopped and turned back toward him. She put her hand on his. She left it there for a while.

"Please, find out who did this."

He nodded. She planted a fast kiss on his cheek and slid out of the car. He sat there for a moment, unconsciously touching his face with his fingertips.

◇◇◇

The rest of the afternoon was spent doing errands. Lowell had dinner alone. It was after nine when the detective returned to his office. He entered the dark reception area and turned on the lamp on Sarah's desk. He then went into his private office, flipped on the overhead lights, adjusted the dimmer until the room had a soft yellowy glow, and closed the door. He went into the bathroom and started to run a bath. Next he took the pillows off the sofa and opened the bed. At the bar, he opened a small refrigerator and took out a bottle of Lowenbrau and a chilled pilsner glass, opened the beer, and slowly poured the contents into the glass.

He printed out a half dozen charts and took them and the beer into the bathroom with him. After he'd settled into the oversized tub he flipped a hinge to release a dropdown that swung across the tub. He placed the beer and the charts on top and carefully scrutinized the papers.

He made a few notations on each chart and put them down. He was tired. He moved the beer and the charts to a small table next to the tub and secured the bath-table back onto the wall. Then he sank down into the tub and lay there for fifteen minutes, recalling Vivian's touch.

When his body felt relaxed enough for sleep, he exited the tub, dried off, and went to sleep on the pull-out couch.

Chapter Four

When his phone rang at eight, the detective was already on his second cup of coffee and working diligently at his computer.

"It's Roland," said the weary voice on the other end. "A few interested parties are coming to see you this afternoon. I was wondering how two o'clock looks."

"I don't have to…"

"Oh yes you do," interrupted the policeman. "I'm afraid there's more involved than you can imagine. You can expect to receive three visitors today."

"Who am I, Ebenezer Scrooge?"

"Whatever. Just please be there at two."

◇◇◇

Sarah came in at nine, replaced the flowers on her desk with a new bouquet and knocked on the detective's door. Sticking her head in she said, "Morning."

Lowell was still in his pajamas, bathrobe, and slippers. Unsurprised, Sarah awaited instructions.

"Sarah, I'm going to need Mort on this case. Would you please call him and see when he can come back from Florida?"

"Sure boss. Can I get you anything for breakfast?"

"Where are you ordering from?"

"I thought Louie's on the corner of 33rd. They make nice pancakes."

Louie's was his favorite restaurant, run by an old hippie from Vermont, who had inherited the building and decided to move his restaurant to Manhattan. He used only organic produce and had a large vegetarian section on his menu.

"Good idea, make mine blueberry. And get me some Stripple."

"How can you eat that phony bacon?" She made a face.

"Because I choose not to eat animals. I thought you and Rudy were going away for the weekend?"

"He can't get off until tomorrow afternoon, so you're stuck with me until then. I'll call in the order."

"I'm going to shower and dress. Buzz me when the food arrives."

She closed the door.

Soon he and Sarah sat on the couch and ate.

"How are things with Rudy?"

"Oh, you know. He's a little, uh, tough to handle sometimes."

Lowell nodded and said nothing.

"I don't know, there are times when I think I'd be better off without him, but I really don't like to be alone."

Sarah was pretty, maybe more than pretty, but she didn't know it. She had a cherub face, round-cheeked and fresh. Her bright red hair was striking. As a secretary she was top notch. Her files were always in order and up to date, Lowell's calendar current, and most of the clients liked her. Her sharp sense of humor was a further plus, and a strong ego. And she was smart.

"Would you like me to look at your charts?"

She perked up. "Oh, would you? But I hate to bother you, especially when you're in the middle of a case."

He waved his hand. "And what good are you to me when you're upset?"

He went back to his desk and pulled up the Solar Fire software. "Here you are, March 26th 1983, at 11:53 a.m., New York City." He printed out the charts. "We've discussed some of this before, of course, but you must be aware of who you are in order to make the most of your opportunities. Relationships can be difficult for you. Your Cancer rising sign makes you very sensitive. With Capricorn ruling your 7th house of relationships, you get very attached to the past, and can find it difficult to get out of a relationship, even if it isn't serving you any longer."

She nodded.

"Over the next few weeks, transiting Jupiter will conjunct your Venus in Taurus, ruler of your 3rd house of communication and your 8th house of sexuality. You can expect some good changes in your social life very soon."

The reading made her feel better, as they always did. She cleaned up, and then returned to her desk and the job of shielding her boss from the outside world. The rest of the day was taken up with phone calls and paperwork.

◇◇◇

Sarah was on the phone with her sister when the door to the office opened and three middle-aged men entered.

"So what did he say then?" She gave a fleeting look at the men. "Uh huh, yeah, and then what?" She glanced up again. There was something familiar about them. What was it? Her sister was rambling on about her boyfriend.

"I've got to call you back. There are some people in the office."

She hung up the phone and smiled her best smile. "How can I help you?"

"We'd like to see Mr. Lowell," said the shortest of the three.

"Do you have an appointment?"

"Yes. Lieutenant Roland spoke with him."

"Okay. Whom shall I say is here?"

"Just tell him Mr. Simpson and friends."

She was about to pick up the phone when recognition hit her. "Oh my god, do you know who you are? I mean, of course you do. And he's…"

The three laughed.

"Oh," Sarah was certain she was blushing. "I'm sure that's alright. Just let me tell him that you're here." She pushed the intercom button and picked up the phone.

"Mr. Lowell, there are some men here to see you...If I'm not completely hallucinating, Pete Simpson, Bobby James, and Barron Dickens...Okay, I'll send them in."

They went through the door into the inner office. Lowell was behind his desk staring at the computer. "Gentlemen, have a seat, please."

They sat in a semi-circle around the desk.

Diminutive Pete Simpson, one-half of Simpson and Goodberry, the most popular duo since the Everly Bothers. Keyboardist and songwriter Bobby James, grown a bit rotund in middle age.

And Barron Dickens. Dressed in black, with his cowboy hat and goatee, he finally fit the role of American poet laureate. He seemed too young when he wrote his early masterpieces. Back then he looked like a kid pretending to be angry at a life he hadn't lived long enough to develop such rage. Now he actually looked better, more in character.

Lowell led off. "Lieutenant Roland told me to expect you. So what brings you here? I have three murders to solve and it's been a busy day."

"Well," said Bobby, "that's why we're here. Since all the murders have happened here and we're all New York musicians, we figured we'd lend a hand."

The detective frowned. "You do realize that since you are most likely all targets, it hardly makes my job easier to have you around."

Pete Simpson chimed in. "Actually, we haven't seen each other in years but we thought it would be better to have us all in the same place for a while. That way you wouldn't have to wonder where we are."

Lowell put his fingers to his chin. "I don't want to have to, um..."

"Look," said Bobby, "if you think you have to baby sit us, let me tell you, there's nothing anyone can throw at us that's tougher than living on the road with a rock band."

Pete's turn. "Besides, it's our asses on the line. We all cleared our schedules for today to see if we could help out. You don't think we're going to hide away with our tails between our legs, do you?"

Barron quietly watched his two musical associates.

"Well," said Lowell, "I doubt that any of you would listen to my advice anyway. At least let me look over your charts to see if there are any violent or dangerous aspects."

Barron cleared his throat. "You know, we talked about seeing you, and frankly, we're a bit scared that one of us may be next. Your reputation precedes you. We can't argue with success."

"I'll take that as a compliment. Give me a moment."

Because of their renown, all three charts were already in the detective's computer files. Many famous people's birth information was included in the Solar Fire computer software programs. He pulled up the chart for each of his distinguished guests, after first double checking the information with each, and printed them on a bi-wheel with the day's transits on the outside. This gave him an opportunity to see the activity affecting each.

As he perused the charts and made some notes on each, the three became restless and wandered about the office. Dickens was particularly fascinated by Buster and Keaton, who in turn seemed interested in him as well. They remained on the rock for the longest time playing peek-a-boo with his fingers. Maybe they knew these hands had written some of the best poetry of a generation. Or maybe he just smelled like food. Who knows with turtles?

"What are your turtles' names?"

"Buster and Keaton."

The poet grinned. "Which is Buster?"

"The one with the red stripe across the face."

"And which one is the boy?"

"Keaton."

"How can you tell?" Dickens lifted Keaton and scrutinized his anatomy.

"The boys have longer nails on the front feet than the girls. It helps them hold on during sex when the female decides she's had enough."

"Ain't much difference between the species, is there? So why turtles?"

"I got tired of burying my dogs."

Dickens nodded.

Pete Simpson was looking at the bookcase. It was divided into two sections. The left side was exclusively astrology books. There must have been several hundred. The right side was a combination of fiction, history, and other assorted tomes as varied as the culture. He thought it was funny that sitting next to each other were *The Invisible Man* by H. G. Wells and *The Invisible Man* by Ralph Ellison. The two books were so different and yet so similar. He looked for other pairings Lowell had made on the shelves.

"To the best of your knowledge, did any of the victims have financial difficulties?"

"You'd have to ask their business managers," said Bobby, "but I assume they were very well off. In fact, I know Gene and Freddie each took out a Bowie bond a few years ago for millions each. I don't know about Wally."

"What's a Bowie bond?" Lowell hadn't heard of them.

Bobby grinned. "It started with David Bowie back in the nineties, that's how it got its name. These big shot bankers created a bond for Bowie, and they raised money against the future royalties of his catalogue. Then a lot of other acts got into it, including Gene and Freddie. They were very popular for a while. So, no, I think they were all very well set."

"Future royalties? You mean people put up millions of dollars against what their records might be worth?"

"Yeah, crazy isn't it?"

"Did any of you take a bond out?"

"Me?" said Bobby, "Nah, I don't run around with an entourage like these other guys do, or did. You know how much money some rock stars spend in a month? It would make you sick. But Gene tried to talk me into it once, that's how I know he and Freddie did it."

"How about you two?" He turned toward Dickens and Simpson.

"None of us has the flare for attention Gene, Wally, and Freddie had," replied Pete. "Besides, we three are very wealthy from the publishing, and that's where the money is, you know, in the publishing. Or at least it used to be."

Lowell held up several pieces of paper. "I find nothing in any of your charts to indicate that you will be killed in the next few days, so I suppose you can hang around while I look into things."

"Well," Dickens grinned, "that's a relief."

"How accurate are you?" asked Bobby.

"Accurate enough."

"Okay," said Simpson, "what's first?"

"I want to interview several people, beginning with the bartender who served Freddie his last drink."

"Where are you seeing her?"

"At her job."

"Great." Simpson hopped up, ready to go like a little kid. "Let's do it."

Chapter Five

They left the building with the detective leading the way. Andy was waiting ever patiently by the limo, and nodded respectfully at his renowned passengers. Lowell winked at Andy before getting in. "Third Avenue and 83rd Street, please."

As the limo made its way uptown, the three rockers discussed politics, music, and the long-term effects of the 60s. Pete and Bobby thought it was the most important cultural phenomenon in modern history. Only Dickens played it down, calling it much ado about nothing.

"In fifty years they'll forget all about us."

"How can you say that?" Bobby seemed sincerely upset.

"Because that's the way it is. Music stars, movie stars, superstars, politicians, what's the difference? There will never be anyone as huge and important to movies as Charlie Chaplin. Go into a Blockbuster's and ask someone under the age of thirty for a Chaplin film. If he ever heard of him he probably couldn't name a single one of his movies.

"Man, things have changed so much already. The new stars are all invented. There's no room for originality anymore, that's a thing of the past. How long do you think I would last on American Idol?"

Lowell listened to this debate with bemusement. Clearly the three had kicked around the topic before. Legacy, relevance. Something those who had lived in the limelight seemed especially worried about. That, and losing their hair.

◇◇◇

At 83rd Street Andy pulled over to the curb. They entered Cantaloupe's Bar and Grill and sat at the otherwise empty bar. Lowell had hoped to have this meeting before happy hour, just him and the bartender. Now, he led an entourage.

The door to the kitchen opened and an attractive middle-aged blonde came out. When she saw the four of them sitting there she was about to tell them the bar wasn't opened yet when Bobby said: "Kitty, is that you?"

She looked for a moment. "Bobby? Bobby James, come here." She scurried over and threw her arms around his neck.

Bobby turned to the other two. "You guys know Kitty, don't you?"

"I knew a Kitty many years ago," said Pete.

"Yeah," chuckled Dickens, "I remember a Kitty. You mean this is Kitty?"

"I know," she said, "father time is a bitch."

Dickens hugged her. "Not for you. You look great. We look like hell."

"You, always the sweet talker. But thank you." Kitty went around to her side of the bar.

She took in Lowell. "I like the ponytail. A good look for you. You could be their manager, but I bet you're the astrologer detective Lieutenant Roland told me about."

He nodded. "Yes, I've been retained to look into the matter. And since you were the last person to see Freddie…"

"Except for the murderer," she interjected.

"Of course, except for the murderer. I thought it would be a good place to start."

"And what are the Three Musketeers doing here?" She smiled at the three.

"They're helping."

She laughed. "Sure they are. So guys, a beer or something stronger? No, I bet it's seltzers with lime."

Barron laughed and nodded.

Kitty turned toward the detective. "You should have seen them in their heyday."

"So," said Lowell, "tell me about the night Freddie died."

"I told the police." She stood a glass of seltzer in front of each.

"Well, tell me."

She went over the events from the time Freddie entered the bar until he left several hours later.

"Did he recognize you?"

"Oh I made him remember." Her laugh filled the room.

"Did you see anyone who might have put something in his drink?"

"When you're bartending with a crowd three deep you don't have time to notice much. I wish I'd spotted something."

"You can't blame yourself," said Pete. "There wasn't anything you could have done."

"He's right," said Bobby.

"Well," she continued, "Freddie left about eleven. I remember some guy with a European accent leaving shortly after, but I don't know if he even went in the same direction as Freddie."

"Can I have your birth information?"

Kitty laughed. "You think I killed Freddie?"

"I don't know who did, but right now nobody is above suspicion."

"Sure. I was born July 16th, 1950, just about 3:20 a.m. according to my mother, right here in New York City."

"Thank you."

"You're not going to write that down?"

"I have an excellent memory."

"Hey, I'm getting hungry," blurted out Bobby.

"There's a surprise." Pete gave his old friend a light punch on the shoulder.

Kitty produced several bowls of bar nuts and pretzels. "Sorry, guys, the kitchen doesn't open for another hour. This okay with you high rollers?"

Bobby grabbed a handful.

"Listen, I have to get some things ready in the back. It was great to see you all again. Stop in one night. I work Friday through Monday." She blew them each a kiss and headed toward the kitchen.

The three stars chimed in like schoolboys. "Bye, Kitty. Great to see you too."

Lowell took out his iPad. "Okay, gents, I'm sure you have other places to be. Let's wrap up our little escapade. Can any of you think of anyone who would want the three of them dead?"

"Except for Gene, I can't think of many who didn't," said Pete. "Rock 'n roll isn't the nicest of businesses and Freddie and Wally weren't the nicest guys."

"Can we narrow it down a bit from the entire human race?"

"Let me think," said Bobby. "I did a tour with Freddie once. He really was a pig in every sense of the word. So I guess maybe one of the girls he used or a boyfriend, something like that?"

"He said he didn't want to include the entire human race, remember?" said Pete.

"Is there anyone who might have had a more personal relationship with any of them?"

"Freddie fired his road manager once," said Bobby, "and it was ugly. But he got with another band soon after. I don't think the guy would kill him."

"Hey, how about that piano player?" asked Pete. "Remember that whole incident on tour? Where was that, Philly, Boston?"

"Buffalo," said Dickens. "That's where it happened, as if playing in that city isn't enough torture."

"*What* happened?" asked Lowell.

"Oh boy," said Pete, "that was some business."

"Yeah," said Bobby, "the fight, the cops, the threatened lawsuit, whew, what a mess."

"So what happened?" asked an exasperated Lowell.

"I'll tell you what happened. Freddie threw him off stage and nearly killed him."

"Oh yeah," said Pete, "it was in all the trades. What was his name? Mark, Mike, something like that."

"Marty," said Bobby.

"Yeah," said Pete, "Marty, uh, Marty…Winebeck, that's it, Marty Winebeck."

"So, *what happened?*" asked Lowell, yet again.

"It was the eighties," started Bobby. "Freddie had hired Marty to play keyboards on the Rocket Fire tour. In those days Freddie and the boys were real party animals. After a show they would return to their hotel with broads, booze, and a big bag of cocaine."

"They were thrown out of hotels in every major city in the world," added Pete.

"Yeah," continued Bobby, "they made the rest of us look like saints. Anyway, one night in Buffalo, Freddie got way too stoned before a gig. They had to drag him away from four naked girls and out of his hotel room. By the time he got on stage he was pissed off and wasted. The concert started all right, and for a few songs Freddie kept it together. Then he started to crash. A doctor was usually kept on retainer who would administer one or another substance to level him off, at least long enough to finish the gig. But this time I guess there wasn't anyone paying attention, and about the fifth song or so Freddie stopped singing. The band kept playing through the song while Freddie meandered around the stage. Then he went over to Marty, who he never liked anyway, and started busting his balls."

"How?" asked Lowell.

"Well, you know, he started by sticking his tongue out and putting his hands up into Marty's face. Marty tried to ignore him, which just made Freddie madder. Finally he kicked the legs out from under Marty's electric piano and the thing collapsed on the stage. The band stopped and a hush fell over the auditorium. Then Freddie smacked Marty in the face, hard. When he went to smack him a second time, Marty put up his hands and defended himself.

"He turned to walk off the stage and Freddie grabbed him from behind and threw him off the stage, about eight feet, I would think. Marty broke his leg, and I think a collar bone or rib or something. The concert was cancelled and that was the last anyone ever heard of Marty."

"Wow, that's quite a story," said Lowell. "How did Freddie get away with it?"

"The power of rock and roll," said Bobby. "They took Marty to the hospital and the cops were called. They interviewed Marty and Freddie and decided it was an internal problem within the band. They didn't find enough evidence, so they said, to warrant a criminal investigation. My guess is that the chief of police was driving a new car within a few weeks."

"Huh, so if everyone knew it was Freddie's fault, why did it hurt Marty's career?"

"Because Freddie had a lot of clout back then, and this business is a lot smaller than you would think. Most of the New York acts had known each other for years. Nobody wanted to get in the middle of a feud with Freddie, so they didn't hire Marty anymore. "

"If I remember correctly," interjected Pete, "I think he was set to play with Redfish after his leg healed, and Freddie stopped it."

"That's right," continued Bobby. "Wally refused to hire him at the last minute. Marty tried to sue Freddie, but it didn't go anywhere."

Lowell tapped in some notes on his iPad. "Marty Winebeck, any of you know where I can reach him?"

They all shrugged.

"Look," said Dickens, "I'd love to play cops and robbers, but I want to get back upstate and play some music. Working on an album."

"Yeah," said Bobby, "I've got to get out to the Island. We're expecting company."

Pete looked at Dickens. "You have a name for the album yet?"

"*City Lights.*" He beamed. "Chaplin's best film."

"Listen," interjected Lowell, "there may be questions I need to ask you guys."

"No problem," said Dickens. "Here's my cell number."

The other two also gave him numbers.

They each made a quick phone call and within fifteen minutes three private cars had swept them off in different directions.

Lowell watched them drive off, relieved. Free to work on his own again, he made for his nearby townhouse, straight to the kitchen. Cold beer and chilled glass in hand, he then parked himself in his favorite chair in the living room. In the past he would have headed for his basement office, but now, with his IPad, he could work anywhere in comfort.

He tapped in the name Marty Winebeck and hit Enter. There was a botanist named Marty Winebeck, and someone in the Caribbean who ran a resort. But no music man.

Chapter Six

The long, summer holiday weekends in Manhattan have a surreal quality about them. While Times Square would be packed with tourists, neighborhood streets are deserted. Restaurants and bars are empty. There are no lines for the movies. You can leisurely dine al fresco at the café of your choice. And shopping in the supermarkets is a relative pleasure, except for the prices and the lack of choices.

As Marty Winebeck walked along the empty sidewalks toward the subway it occurred to him, not for the first time, that this is what the city would look like after a plague, lots of real estate and not a lot of bodies to fill it. *If the bird flu came I could probably get a real deal on a one-bedroom*, he chuckled to himself, *assuming I survived.*

This was a long weekend. This year July 4th fell on a Tuesday. Today was Monday and anyone who could get away with it was taking off today as well. It was a four day mini-holiday, five for those who played hooky on Friday. It was a very long weekend.

Manhattan on a holiday weekend could be the most wonderful time, if you had money and people to spend it with. But Marty was broke and had very few friends. A musician's life consists mostly of work, recovering from work, or looking for work. It often took longer to land a gig than most of them lasted. If you found steady employment you held on to it for dear life.

Marty had been luckier than most musicians. Every summer for seven years he had played a weekend job in the Hamptons where he would pick up lots of private parties to supplement his income, a musician's paradise. He had no contract with the club, so every spring he held his breath to see if they were hiring him back, and every spring they had, until this year. A new owner had brought his own piano player with him.

It was the summer that had supported most of the rest of the year. He was able to survive the autumn in New York City, a less than fruitful time for live acts, if he was careful about spending his summer income. By Thanksgiving, Christmas parties would be booked and he could usually make it through the long, cold winter, living off the remnants of the holidays, just barely surviving until the summer began. How was he going to make it until Christmas? He couldn't make it through July.

He got on the Lexington Avenue subway at 86th Street and headed downtown. It was hot, ninety degrees plus, and humid as hell. The station was empty. The train was sparsely occupied, but delightfully air-conditioned.

He reluctantly left the refreshing train at the 28th Street station and walked through the steamy heat over to 30th Street and 8th Avenue, entered a Starbucks and ordered a tall, meaning small, drip. He handed the girl two dollar bills and received nine cents change. He put the change into the tip container and took his coffee to the condiment stand. There he added two packets of sugar in the raw and some milk, stirred it all together and took a sip. He then took about a dozen more sugar packets and a large wad of Starbucks napkins and put them in them in his shoulder bag. It was the only coffee in New York that gave him the kick he needed. It galled him every time to lay out that much money, but if he was going to pay two dollars for a cup of coffee he wasn't leaving empty-handed.

He took his coffee and headed out the door, turned right and continued down 30th Street. He entered a nondescript building and walked through the lobby to a doorway in the back. He pushed an intercom, waited until the buzzer sounded to let him through the door and down a flight of stairs to Mars Recording Studios. This area of Manhattan had once been the center of recording and rehearsal studios, but rapidly rising rents and conversions of commercial buildings into condos had depleted the supply. Mars Studio was one of the few remaining from the old days. Their lease still had five years to go.

"Hi, Eddie."

Eddie, the engineer and owner, was busy setting up the studio for their recording session. Marty had cut a deal to do all their in-house keyboard work in exchange for cheap studio time so he could record his own tunes. This was one of his sessions to work on original material.

Eddie was on his back underneath the board plugging things in. "Hey, Marty. Did you see the paper today?"

"No. I'm trying to quit."

Eddie laughed. "Well, I think you should look at this one." He pointed to the table across the room.

Marty stood up and walked across the room, coffee in hand. He picked up the *Post* and opened it to the headline. "Freddie Gets Fingered," the rag said, in all its subtlety and style. He sat down and read the story.

"Holy crap."

Eddie stood up and twisted a few dials. "Didn't you know him?"

"Yeah, since high school."

"Jesus, ain't that something? So, what do you think?" Eddie gave Marty the 'okay' sign pointing toward the piano.

"I think it was twenty-five years too late," he replied under his breath.

Marty entered the recording room, sat at the Yamaha piano, and put on his headphones.

"Sing a little for me so I can set the levels."

Marty put his hands on the keys and suddenly felt very much in control. It was a feeling he'd gotten all his life, whenever he played. He hadn't been very good at sports, and was always a thin, un-macho type. His childhood was ruthless, constant ribbing from the other kids, a real outcast. It wasn't until his eighteenth year that he began playing music seriously. The piano bench was the only place he felt truly at home and completely alive.

He sang a few lines until Eddie interrupted him. "That's fine. What are you recording?"

"It's something new. Put it on the disc for the musical."

Marty, like many artists, worked on several projects at a time. When inspiration or money was around you had to be ready to take advantage of the circumstances and move the venture forward. One of the ongoing projects was "The Musical," an original idea about the music business, time travel, and the baby boomers, that he had been writing and rewriting for about a decade. It was close to finished. All he needed was lots and lots of money. At least his deal with the studio allowed him to record demos of the score, which he hoped he could use to entice potential investors. Even with serious backing putting together a musical was a long, tiring, daunting road that not many had succeeded in transiting. Without money you're pretty much pissing in the wind.

Marty played an F Major chord then he began to sing:

"I came into this dream
Such a long time ago
It's hard to believe
I'm as old as I am…"

◇◇◇

At a quarter to five they wrapped up the session. Eddie made a rough copy of the work they had done that day so Marty could review it. He handed the CD to the singer and they said goodbye.

It was still hot with no breeze or shade. The streets were even more deserted than they had been in the early afternoon. Everyone who hadn't left the city last night had scooted away today.

He walked over to the East Side and started up Park Avenue. At 38th Street he walked over to a phone booth and, after carefully scrutinizing his surroundings, took a tiny metal object and a small medicine container from his pocket. He opened the container, tipped a small amount of a reddish-green substance into the metal object, and then returned the container to his pocket. Looking around once more he took a lighter from the same pocket, picked up the pay phone pretending to speak into it, and lit the substance. He inhaled a healthy amount of smoke, looked around once more, and then exhaled. He repeated the procedure twice more, and started walking north. It was strong pot with an earthy taste that reminded him of the seventies. But then lately, everything was reminding him of the seventies, including the economy. The THC did its job. He felt the small of his back relax and he walked at a steady, slow pace, controlling his breathing as he went.

At 89th Street he turned east and headed toward his fourth floor walk-up between York and East End. It was repressively hot in the studio apartment. He clicked on the TV, turned on the air conditioner to the energy-save setting, and sat on the couch/bed.

When he had cooled off enough to feel somewhat normal he opened his shoulder bag and took out the copy of the *Post*. It always had the most outrageous headlines. "Freddie Got Fingered" ranked right up there with the best.

He carefully cut the front page off and opened a portfolio he kept in the coffee table drawer. He opened the book to a blank page, slid the *Post's* front page into the plastic folder, and smoothed it out.

He closed the book and then reopened it to the first page and the first victim, Gene Hallow, front man for Rapid Rising, a soft rock band from the eighties known mostly for sweet syrupy ballads. That *Post's* headline read: "Gene Finally Gets Laid," in reference to one of his biggest hit, the atypical slightly raunchy, "When I'm Laid to Rest." There's a line in the song that goes:

> *The greatest lay of all*
> *I said upon request*
> *Is not a girl at all*
> *But when I'm laid to rest*

He flipped to the second page. Wally Fischer, known to the world as Redfish, was the second victim. A singer-songwriter with a twisted political point of view, Redfish spewed violence and anger from his mouth long before rap made it commonplace. If you called him Wally to his face he would leap at you with both fists flailing. He was an angry middle-aged boy, mad at the world and his parents. Neurotic and petulant, he demanded full attention wherever he went.

Not many people liked Wally. That was what groupies and gofers were for. But he did sell a hell of a lot of records, and anyone who fed the star-maker machine was good for everybody, so they put up with Wally.

At least until a month ago when somebody stabbed him to death. Nobody who knew him was terribly upset when Wally died, except perhaps his manager and agent, both of whom were about to take a serious pay cut. The press had never really liked him, and they had a field day taking his lyrics out of context and twisting them all around. Wally's headline in the *Post*: "The Deepest Cut of All."

And Freddie made three.

He stared at Freddie's headline for a long time. Then he smiled a sad grin, closed the book and put it in the table drawer. He went to his woefully out-of-date Dell computer and opened his email. He wrote a short message, attached it to eight separate blind copy email addresses, printed a copy, and sent it out.

The note simply said: "Freddie's gone. Three down and one to go."

Chapter Seven

The fourth of July is the quietest day in the city, with the possible exception of Christmas. Lowell fed the turtles and then walked over to Louie's for breakfast. It was now eight and already the temperature was in the eighties. He had been forced to forego his usual turtleneck and wore a black t-shirt. He was their only customer and sat outside at one of the four tables, leisurely reading the *Times* while he ate. After breakfast he strolled around the neighborhood for a while, but it was already too hot for a long walk.

He often spent the day leisurely meandering through the distinct neighborhoods. Years ago he would wind his way around the historic streets of Tribeca, Soho, Chinatown, Little Italy, the Village, and end up in Gramercy Park near his office. Each had its own flavor, a dozen villages within a city. But all that was disappearing.

Where you used to see little old ladies sitting on their stoops exchanging neighborhood gossip and recipes, now there were young upwardly mobile couples in $200 jeans rushing to make their first million.

Only Chinatown kept its unique style, and even that was beginning to change. Hipster leisure bars were popping up in storefronts where immigrants had toiled for centuries.

He returned to the office. He had given Sarah time off so she and Rudy could enjoy a few days on Long Island. She wouldn't be back until tomorrow. His assistant, Mort, was still in Florida taking care of family business, and the office seemed particularly empty.

He showered and closed up the sofa bed. Then he turned on his computer and opened the Solar Fire astrology program. He brought Freddie's chart on screen, and then printed it. He took the paper and paced back and forth across the room, stopping occasionally to pet the turtles, both of whom seemed aware of his agitation. They stayed out on their rock a long time, until he finally sat back down at his desk. Then Buster and Keaton slowly returned to the water.

This was where he did his real work. This was why people paid him. Any idiot could tail someone or photograph them coming out of a motel room. What he did that other detectives couldn't do was look at these pieces of paper and recognize where to seek his solution. He picked up Freddie's chart and walked over to the turtles. Buster was sitting on a rock looking up at him with anticipation.

"Freddie was born August 9th, 1948, at 6:05 a.m. at Doctor's Hospital in Manhattan," he told the turtle. "This is a commanding chart. There are three planets close together, that's called a stellium, in the 12th House in Leo. Mercury, Pluto, and the Sun are in close conjunction, with the Sun almost exactly on the ascendant. This made Freddie quite charismatic. It also made him a control freak, with tremendous personal power. Although with the Mercury and Pluto in the 12th House he was quite capable of hiding his true motivations and intentions. Venus, ruler of the career house, was in sextile to the mid-heaven, an aid to a successful career, which certainly was the case."

Buster was fascinated.

"There is also a second stellium in Libra involving Neptune, Mars, and the Moon. It shows a strong talent for music, and an interesting and strong relationship with the public. It also shows that while Freddie was able to control much of his reality through the Pluto – Sun – Mercury connection, in truth, with Mars so close to Neptune, his ego was not very strong, and he overcompensated for his internal fears through his outward manipulation. None of this knowledge can help Freddie anymore. Perhaps it might help identify his killer."

He punched in the birth information of the other two victims and showed them to Buster. "At the time of their deaths, Wally and Freddie's charts showed heavy transits by Mars, the most aggressive of planets, and Pluto, ruler of hidden agendas and vengeance, both of which one would expect to find in violent murder charts. But, they were not very prominent in Gene's chart at the time of his death. Jupiter, however, was active in all three." Buster nodded. "It's considered the "lucky" planet, the planet of growth and optimism, of expansion, higher education, and long journeys. And I have found that description to be very accurate in my years of studies."

He also knew how often Jupiter appeared in an active role in death charts and had long ago realized the obvious. *Death is a long journey of expansion that most likely offers us some higher educational potential. Perhaps death was more Jupiter's domain than was commonly recognized,* he thought, *and maybe we shouldn't be so pessimistic about it.*

"All three charts point toward a financial situation with violent undertones. There were difficult transits upon the ruler of the 2nd house of money in each. What was the connection? And why were Mars and Pluto active in Wally's and Freddie's charts, but not in Gene's."

The phone rang a little after three. He was going to ignore it when he noticed the number on caller ID. He picked it up. "Hi there. How are you holding up?"

"I'm okay." Vivian's voice sounded a little strained. "I was wondering if you were free this evening. I'd like to get out for a few hours and don't really feel like being with show biz people, if you know what I mean."

"I'll pick you up at seven and we'll get some dinner."

"No, I feel like taking a long walk. I'll meet you at your office."

"Okay. If you like we can catch the fireworks at nine."

"Ooh, that would be fun."

He told her the address and hung up. Then he called the Four Seasons and made a reservation. Normally there was a long wait for a table, but the manager was an astrology client whom Lowell had helped during a time of great distress.

A little before seven there was a knock on the office door. He opened it. She was dressed simply, but elegantly, in a light blue blouse and white pants. Except for a pair of diamond stud earrings and two rings she was otherwise unadorned.

"So, this is where you do your magic. Show me around?"

"This is the reception area." He stated the obvious. "Sarah sits here. There's another office for Mort, my assistant, and a small conference room with a client's bathroom over there." Then he opened the door to his inner sanctum. "This is my office and part time home."

"You live here?"

"Sometimes. I have a home uptown, but when I'm in the middle of an ongoing investigation I hate to be interrupted, so I'll stay here for a few days at a time. The couch opens to a king-size mattress, and I have a full bathroom."

He opened the door and showed her the bathroom and dressing area, complete with walk-in closet and mirrors.

She walked around the room taking it all in. She stopped by the tank and was introduced to Buster and Keaton, who seemed to enjoy her immensely.

"What's in the cabinets?"

"I'll show you." He walked to his desk and picked up the universal remote. He pushed a few buttons and two TVs came on – one set to CNBC, and the other to CSPAN.

"Wow. That's quite a setup you've got."

"I need every weapon in my arsenal. The ancient and the most modern come together to give me the answers I seek."

They caught a cab to the restaurant on East 52nd Street, although Lowell had his car and driver waiting for them later. There wouldn't be a free cab anywhere after the fireworks.

Dinner was excellent. Vivian had chipotle tuna. Lowell had the ravioli, and for dessert they each had the crème brulee. They discussed art, politics, music, and movies, and found that they agreed on most things. When they disagreed it wasn't so much an ideological difference as a generational or cultural clash.

They left the restaurant and headed toward the Hudson River. As they walked west they were joined by a crowd that continued to grow. It was as if the entire island had been tipped and all the people were spilling over toward the river.

They reached the West Side Highway and took their place among the throngs eager to see the show. The crowd and the darkness provided Vivian with the anonymity she needed.

At nine o'clock exactly the display began. The sky lit up in a spectacular display of pyrotechnics. Like little children the crowd gasped and applauded the show.

After a half hour they had had their fill.

"Maybe we should leave a little early and beat the crowd," said Lowell.

"Could we walk for a few blocks?"

"Of course."

His driver, Andy, was sitting half a block down from the drive. When he saw them he started the car. Lowell made a walking motion with his fingers. Andy nodded.

"I never spent too much time in New York City," she said. "I grew up in California and went to school in Boston. It's a bit overwhelming, isn't it?"

"It can be."

"It's a beautiful night." She slipped her arm around his.

"A little warm, though." He felt a little tongue-tied, which was quite unusual for the astrologer.

"David, I need to head back to the hotel. I have an early appointment tomorrow with the organizers of my dad's memorial service. I need to pull this together before all of his friends and associates leave for the Hamptons or the Vineyard for the rest of the summer. You'll come with me to the service, yes? "

"Of course." Lowell knew Andy would be close by with the car, and he was. The limo pulled up, and they got in.

He was sorry to end the evening. He had found her intel-
ligent and incredibly attractive, and was just happy to be in her
presence. "The Carlyle, please, Andy."

"Right away, boss."

Vivian had been in her share of limousines, but this one
was as much like a living room as any she had ever seen. There
was a TV screen, a small refrigerator, a fold-down desk with a
computer terminal. The usual rich man's toys. But this limo had
two things she had never seen.

"What's that?" She pointed at a computer screen that seemed
to be continuously running a strange program. It showed what
her untrained eye thought was an astrology chart, but it seemed
to be moving. At least the planets did.

"That is an astrolabe. It's been used since the middle ages to
visually depict the positioning of the planets at any given time,
giving the astrologer a clearer picture. It's often used for divination, or fortune telling. Modern astrologers also use it to get a
visual of where the planets are at any moment. It used to be a
mechanical instrument that was turned by hand. Of course, we
have updated the technology, but it's virtually the same thing,
and I use it for the same reason."

She stared at it for a few moments. "I noticed they move at
different speeds."

"Sure, just as the planets do. The closer to the Sun the faster
the motion, except for the Moon which, you will notice," he
pointed to the screen, "moves much quicker than the rest."

"What does the Moon rule?"

"It rules lots of things, particularly our emotions."

She smiled. "And they do move quickly, don't they?"

Lowell hit a button and the windows darkened for a moment.
Then they lit up again, only the scene outside had changed.
They seemed to be driving through a snowy mountainous area.

Vivian put her hand on the window. It was cold to the touch.
And she knew it was almost ninety outside. She pulled her hand
back suddenly.

"What the…?"

Lowell laughed. "That is technology that will be available soon, once the bugs are worked out of it and the licensing agreements are reached. The inventor is an old client of mine. He's been working on this for ten years. Pretty wild, huh?"

"I'll say."

"The screen is a plasma insert that is transparent when turned off. Once you initialize the screen it actually takes on the physical characteristics of whatever program you're running. There are twenty four mini-speakers throughout the car that produce an astoundingly realistic atmosphere, don't you think?"

She touched the screen. It was damp and cold.

"People will have these in restaurants, nightclubs, and at home. Bored? Can't get away? Turn on Miami and make believe. Go ahead, try another one."

"Which one?"

"Where in LA do you live?"

"Just north of Malibu on the ocean."

"Perfect. Why don't you push #7?"

She turned the knob to #7 and pushed the green button. The screen darkened again for a moment, and then they were driving on what she instantly recognized as the Pacific Coast Highway. "Oh my god, this is my neighborhood." She pushed her face against the glass as if trying to look back at the road. "This is just amazing. In five minutes we'll pass my house. It'll be there, won't it?"

Lowell nodded. "These are 3D projections of footage shot about eighteen months ago, so if the building was there then, you'll see it."

"Any chance I'll see myself there?"

"None. The technicians made sure there were no people in the footage, both for legal reasons and because it helps to imagine yourself somewhere if there aren't people to process."

She remained entranced and giggled as they passed her house. She turned to Lowell. "Would you like to join me for a nightcap?"

"I'd be delighted to."

When they got to the Carlyle Andy got out first and went around to open the door. He was six feet three inches tall, and at two hundred ten pounds of muscle, an imposing figure, but that wasn't why Lowell hired him. With a black belt in aikido, Lowell was capable of taking care of himself in most situations, but he knew the limitations of his physical prowess, and powerful back up was very reassuring. Lowell had almost lost his life investigating the Winston case by overestimating his skills. An ex-racecar driver, Andy was the best man to have behind the wheel, not that his size wasn't an added benefit. But it was his sense of humor that ultimately got him the job. His wit was dry and cutting, quite like Lowell's. In fact, they shared a similar view of the world: part cynical, part hopeful. They also shared a strong work ethic, something Lowell demanded of all his employees.

Lowell and Vivian entered the bar and sat at a small table. A pianist was playing "When Sunny Gets Blue." Several couples were sitting intimately. A waitress came up quickly and took their order. She had a Remy, he had a Beck's.

When the drinks came Vivian raised her snifter. "Here's to the discovery of the truth."

Lowell wondered, not for the last time, what uncovering the truth about her father's death would ultimately mean for her.

They knocked their glasses together and each took a sip.

Chapter Eight

The long holiday was finally over. It was Wednesday July fifth and things were starting to return to summertime normal.

Sarah came in at nine, put a new bouquet in the vase on her desk and knocked on the door. It was already over ninety outside, and the air conditioners were on full blast. Her hair was a mess from the heat and she had her brush out, preparing to repair the damage.

"Come in, Sarah."

Holding the brush in one hand she opened the door and entered. "Hey, boss, how about some breakfast?"

Lowell picked his head up from the computer screen. "Yes, that's a good idea."

"What would you like?"

"Something different, you decide." He put his head back down.

Sarah ordered him a Spanish omelet loaded with vegetables and just a bit spicy. When it came to his vegetarian diet Lowell allowed for eggs, if they were organic.

When the food arrived Lowell insisted on hearing all about Sarah's long weekend with Rudy. It had started out okay, she said, but by the second day had deteriorated into their usual arguments. They did make up though, on the way home, and had formed yet another in a long series of truces.

"What you said in the reading still holds?"

He nodded. "You'll understand in a few weeks. For now just stay the course and do what feels right. You'll know what you have to do when the time comes."

After breakfast Sarah called Lieutenant Roland and got the number of Freddie's manager, Larry Latner, called and made an appointment.

◇◇◇

Latner's office was in a private brownstone on West 76th Street between Columbus and Central Park West. It was a medieval looking structure, made of stone and brick, four stories high. There were two entrances, one for the residence and one on the basement level for the business. He went down the four steps and rang the bell.

A tall blonde in a short red skirt answered.

"May I help you?"

"David Lowell. I have an appointment with Mr. Latner."

"Please, walk this way."

"If I could walk that way I wouldn't need the talcum powder," he said, half to himself.

"What?"

"Oh, nothing, just an old joke."

He followed her into the basement of the building, which consisted of a suite of offices complete with a reception area. She pointed toward several chairs.

"Please have a seat and I'll let Mr. Latner know you're here."

He sat and scrutinized the office. There was a desk where a cute woman with dark hair cut in a pageboy sat typing. On the wall hung about a dozen gold and platinum records, all framed and noted. In the magazine-stand next to his chair were copies of *Billboard*, *Cashbox*, and several other trade papers. Not a *Time* or *Newsweek* in sight.

A few moments later the inner door opened and the tall blonde reappeared. "Right this way."

He stood up and followed her into the private office. Once he was inside she disappeared once again.

A short, stocky, man with a terrible comb-over sat behind a large metal desk. He was wearing a black t-shirt and a tan sport coat with a large brownish stain on the lapel.

"Come in, come in." His spoke in a high nasally twang. He stood and extended his hand, which Lowell shook. It was a weak, damp handshake. "Larry Latner. Please, sit down."

"David Lowell." He took a seat, nonchalantly wiping his clammy hand on his pants.

"I understand you're working with the police on Freddie's murder."

Lowell nodded.

"You'll forgive me if I'm a bit abrupt, but we're all shell-socked and in mourning. This is terrible, just terrible. Freddie was like a son to me."

"I completely understand. I'll be as brief as I can. I'm interested in Freddie's life, his friends and enemies, anyone that may have had a reason to kill him."

The manager sat back and smiled. "I'm sure you've heard a lot of stories by now about Freddie and his, uh, shenanigans. Well, let me tell you something. Nobody gets to where Freddie and the band got without stepping on a few toes. Sure, they were wild boys, back in the seventies and eighties, but that's all behind them. We were all kids once, right?"

"Freddie was forty-two when he was arrested for driving his car into the living room of an ex-wife's home," replied Lowell. "I guess adolescence lasts a little longer if you're in the music business."

"Well, yes, it did take Freddie a little longer to grow up, it's true. But he finally got sober and started behaving like an adult. Besides, his talent was its own excuse. Do you know how many records he sold?"

"Is that how you judge talent, by how many records are sold?"

"Well, yes." He popped a handful of M&Ms into his mouth. "This is America. That's exactly how we judge everything."

The intercom buzzed. "Excuse me a moment." Latner picked up the phone. "Yes, what is it? Okay, tell him I'll call him back in fifteen minutes."

He hung up the phone. "Sorry about that."

"So, Freddie may have made a few enemies in his life."

"I suppose so, but then, who among us hasn't?"

"Hmm, yes. Well, I'm also interested in Freddie's economic situation."

"What about it?" He grabbed another handful of M&Ms.

"What sort of shape was he in, financially speaking?"

"Rocket Fire is one of the biggest acts in the world. Their last tour grossed over sixty million dollars. Their last album sold half a million, and their next one is going to be the biggest of their career, unfortunately."

"Why unfortunately?"

"It's because of Freddie's death. The album is due out next week, and we expect it to debut at number one in *Billboard*. It should sell between eight and ten million."

"So Freddie's death is actually good for business?"

"Well, in the short run it is. But of course, without Freddie there is no future. No more tours, no more albums, only reissues and compilations. There are some tracks the band never released that might be put out in the next few years, but for Rocket Fire, that's all she wrote."

"This isn't very good news for you then, is it?"

"You see this townhouse? I own it, along with another in this neighborhood that I bought in the eighties for peanuts. I have a house in Florida and one near Malibu. If I quit the business tomorrow I would still have enough money to live out several lifetimes. I don't need any more. But yes, Freddie's death is certainly going to limit my business."

"What will you do?"

"I do have other acts, and I'll continue to manage Rocket Fire's catalogue and make sure the rest of the boys can continue to make a living. They're like my family. Someone has to look out for them."

"They can still make money?"

"Oh sure. They all own a piece of the records, although not as much as Freddie and Ritchie Polk."

The phone rang again. He picked it up. "What now? Who? Okay, put him on…George, I really can't talk right now…Well, can't it wait? Okay, use the red cover and blue background. With the white lettering we've got it…That's right, red, white, and blue, now you get the picture? …All right I'll call you back."

He hung up. "I'm sorry again, but things are just moving quickly and I can barely keep up. Where were we?"

"You were telling me about Ritchie Polk."

"Ritchie is the guitar player and co-writer of the songs. He and Freddie split the majority of publishing rights, which is where the real money is."

"I've heard that before about publishing rights. Tell me a little about that. How is the money earned?"

"When an artist or a group puts out a record, there are several ways the act can make money. The singer gets a piece of artist's royalties, and sometimes the musicians get a small piece, especially if they are in an ongoing group, such as Rocket Fire. But it is the writer and publisher of those songs who collect most of the money. They each take in a large share of what's called performance and mechanical royalties. These are the most lucrative pieces of any composition.

"The writers and publishers get paid every time a song is played in a concert, on the radio, TV, or movies, and gets picked up in survey. The money is collected through the performance organizations. The largest are ASCAP, short for the American Society of Authors, Composers, and Publishers, and B.M.I., or Broadcast Music Incorporated. Anyone who wishes to broadcast a recording registered with one of these organizations must pay a fee, which is then transferred to the accounts of the writers and publishers.

"With me so far?" He grabbed another handful of M&Ms.

Lowell nodded. "Of course."

"Okay. Mechanical royalties are collected through the Harry Fox Agency, whose purpose is to collect monies owed the artists, writers, and publishers directly from record companies and other vendors. A certain amount is collected for each song on an album based upon how many copies it has sold. They also collect money from movie sales, TV, the Internet, ring tones for cell phones, and any other way a song can generate income.

"These are the two main ways a songwriter makes his money. And if you write hit songs you make a fortune. A song at the top of the charts will be played thousands of times for a few weeks or months, depending upon its popularity, generating hundreds of thousands of dollars of income in a short period of time. Thereafter it continues to create income as it gets picked up by secondary and oldies stations. Some writers have only one hit in their entire careers, but it can produce enough income that, if invested carefully, can last for years."

"And Freddie and Ritchie wrote how many hits?"

"All told they've had thirty-two top ten hits, eleven number ones."

"So Freddie was wealthy when he died?"

"Sure was. Although there was a time in the nineties when his spending surpassed his income and he was cash-poor for a few years."

"That's when he took out the Bowie Bond."

"Oh, you know about that, huh?" He seemed surprised. "Then you know Freddie was set for life no matter what happened in his future."

"And how much was the bond issued for?"

The manager leaned back in his chair and paused for dramatic effect. "Fifty million dollars," he finally said.

"Fifty million. And has it been worth the investment?"

Latner nodded. "I don't pay much attention to it, but I'm sure it has. Do you know how much those songs generate a year, between ASCAP, money from oldies stations, TV, movies, and now the gigantic TV commercial market aimed at the baby-boomers? They're using all the old songs to sell cars, diapers, toilet paper, anything. That bond is as good as gold."

"Well, if you could make a list of anyone you think might have a grudge against Freddie, I would appreciate it."

"Sure, I'll email it to you."

"How about Marty Winebeck?"

"Marty Winebeck, talk about ancient history. How did you even hear about that? I don't even know where Marty Winebeck is, or if he's even alive, do you?"

Lowell shook his head.

"He was just a punk anyway, looking for an excuse to sue Freddie because he couldn't make it on his own. Why? Do you think he's involved in this?"

"I really don't know."

"Well, I wouldn't put it past him. The stink he made, the trouble he cost Freddie and the boys was unbelievable, and all because of a little misunderstanding."

"I heard that it was a bit more than that."

"Oh musicians are all children," said the manager. "They have fights, you patch things up and move on to the next city. You don't sue your friends and bandmates, it's just not done."

The intercom buzzed and Latner picked up the phone. "Tell them to wait just a minute." He hung up. "I'm sorry to cut you short but my one o'clock just got here and I'm swamped with work."

Lowell rose. "That's quite all right, I was finished anyway. Thank you for your time."

On his way through the reception area he passed a group of five long-haired young men in their twenties. *Probably one of the hottest acts in America,* he thought to himself, *and I don't have a clue who they are. Getting old sucks.*

Chapter Nine

Vivian had made the necessary arrangements for Freddie's memorial service, then went back to LA to check on her house, get some fresh clothing, and tie up some business. Although he wouldn't admit it to himself, Lowell missed her.

He had gone over as many details of the case as he could, but needed a break to get perspective. He kept himself busy, talking to his daughter in Dallas several times, reviewing some loose ends from previous cases, and even ran the reservoir in Central Park, like he had promised himself he'd do. He couldn't walk for two days.

Vivian returned the following Friday, the day before the service. Lowell didn't call her, leaving her the peace she would need before an emotional day.

Freddie's funeral was a madhouse.

The streets had been blocked off and nobody was getting near the place without a pass. Andy drove Lowell and Vivian within two blocks, only to be waved away by a policeman standing in front of a yellow barrier.

"Andy, we'll get out here. I'll call you when we're leaving, should be in about an hour."

They walked across the avenue and passed the police barrier, after first displaying their invitations. Normally Lowell would have avoided this at all cost, but he couldn't refuse Vivian's request.

When they reached the front of the funeral chapel the paparazzi attacked Vivian like a minnow in a sea of barracudas. Lowell did his best to keep them at bay, although he couldn't prevent them both from being photographed repeatedly.

But there was plenty of other fodder to keep the gossip mongers busy. Limo after limo was dropping human cargo at the barricade and rock's royalty, wrinkled and otherwise, was in full display. This was, to date, *the* social event of the rock and roll season.

Once they were inside all was calmer. The press was not allowed inside, and cameras were strictly forbidden. The chapel hall was massive, one of the biggest in New York, but it still couldn't hold the throng of fans, friends, and enemies who wished to see Freddie off to his final journey.

It looked like a who's who of show business. Superstars, movie stars, record executives, secretaries, and wannabes crowded the hall. Most of the local politicians had come, more fans of the potential votes than of Freddie's music.

Freddie's grubby manager, Larry Latner, and two other men approached.

"Vivian, how are you? I'm so very sorry. If there's anything I can do for you, anything at all, you know you only have to ask. Your father was like a son to me."

"Thank you, Larry." She hugged him. "I know how close you were to him. This is David Lowell. He's working on the case."

"Yes, I know Mr. Lowell. Any progress?"

"We're following up on a few leads."

"Well, let me know if there's anything I can do for *you* as well."

Vivian touched Lowell's arm. "David, I'm going to find my seat and say hello to a few people."

"Of course. I'll join you in a moment."

Lowell turned and faced the other two gentlemen. One was tall and thin with a childlike face, despite his obvious middle-age. He had long hair, parted in the middle and thinning on top. He wore John Lennon glasses.

The other was much shorter, had a full beard, neatly trimmed, and also wore his hair about shoulder length. They were both dressed in black suits. And they were both trying too hard to look young and hip.

"Oh, forgive me," said Latner. "This is Robert Frey." He motioned toward the tall one, "and Johnny Gleason," he nodded toward the shorter. "Robert is Gene's manager and Johnny is Redfish's manager."

"Do you think Freddie's death is connected to Gene and Wally?" asked Frey.

"I would assume so," said Lowell. "It seems an awfully big coincidence for the three to be murdered, don't you think?"

"I don't know that much about it," replied Frey. "Besides, the police still aren't sure if Gene was murdered or if he fell or jumped from the window, isn't that right?"

"That is technically true, but since Freddie's death they have all been listed as murders."

Gleason nudged Frey.

"Wally's turnout was the biggest."

"You're crazy. Gene's was much bigger."

"You're nuts. What do you think, Larry?"

Latner turned to them. "We're at a funeral, for god's sake. What difference does it make?"

The other two blushed slightly.

"Besides," continued Latner, "I was at both and neither one had nearly as good a turnout as this one."

Frey shook his head. "Gene's was. Don't you remember how many cops they needed?"

"That's because you had Gene's at a small church. Of course it's going to overflow if you put too many people in it. That's like pouring ten ounces of booze into a six ounce glass."

"Do you even know what the hell you're talking about?"

"Well, Freddie was able to get a full house and he was a devout atheist."

"I wonder if he still feels that way?" said Frey, looking up.

"Oh please," said Latner.

"Gentlemen, a pleasure." Lowell tried not to let his sarcasm show.

"Of course. We'll see you after the sho…service."

As he walked away he heard the three managers continue to argue over who's funeral was the best draw.

◇◇◇

Vivian and Lowell sat in the front row. Vivian looked around the room. "I thought for sure my mother would show up. She said she'd consider it. Even though they've been divorced for a long time, I still thought she'd make it. I guess some wounds never heal."

"Give her time," said Lowell. "She must grieve in her own way. Don't forget, she's probably mourning many things today including I'm sure, her own lost youth."

She took hold of his arm. "I'm supposed to say something, but I don't know if I can. This has been all too much for me."

"You do what you can. Everyone will understand."

The service was interesting, to say the least. Whoever wrote the speech that the funeral director read was obviously a big fan. When he mentioned what a great humanitarian Freddie was it took a full minute for the crowd to stop laughing.

The whole thing ran a bit long, with a childhood friend of Freddie's going on forever about their first bikes, girls, and bad behavior. Bobby James was perfect, however, speaking briefly about music, loss, and cruel ends.

Vivian wanted to get up to say something, but when she tried to stand, her emotions overwhelmed her, and she realized she would just fall apart.

When it was over Lowell called Andy and led Vivian down the block to his waiting limousine.

"Andy, would you take Ms. Younger wherever she wishes."

"Sure boss."

"You're not coming?" Vivian didn't hide her disappointment.

"There are a few people I need to talk to here, and frankly I can get it done more discreetly and with less fanfare without you. I'll meet you later, if you'd like."

"Yes. I would like that very much."

As he watched Andy drive her away he wondered once again what uncovering the truth about her father's death might ultimately mean for her.

He walked back to the chapel just in time to run into Bobby James.

"Hey, David," said Bobby. Lowell liked the piano-playing musician.

"Any new thoughts about Freddie's death?" asked Lowell.

"Not really. Nice service though, didn't you think?"

Lowell was looking around at the crowd leaving the chapel. "Any of these people important enough in Freddie's life to be suspects?"

"There's Freddie's second wife over there. I guess she would qualify. Of course he had three, including the current widow."

"And where is *she?*"

"Actually, she's right behind the second one, and it looks like they're both headed over here."

Moments later two women, one blonde, and one brunette, approached.

"Bobby, it's so nice to see you again," said the blonde.

She was about forty, tall and beautiful with a powerful persona, something the astrologer found quite common in the show business clique.

Lowell knew all about her. She was a model when they married, had two children with Freddie and, after their divorce, one with a film director she never married. She lived quite nicely on the money she received in her divorce from Freddie. Now that he was dead her children stood to inherit a great deal more. They were eight and six, so of course she would have control of it for many years.

"Hello, Tracy," said Bobby. "How are things?"

She came over to him, tried to put her arms around his ample waist, pulling him in for a very intimate kiss, thought Lowell.

The brunette gave Bobby a kiss on the cheek.

"Hi, Rose," he said. "Are you holding up okay?"

"I'll survive."

She was shorter than Tracy, about five six, but just as beautiful. Her dark features were magnetic, tantalizing, and forbidding at the same time.

Lowell knew about her as well. A struggling actress who specialized in soft-core horror films, their relationship had begun while Freddie was still married to Tracy. Although still legally married at the time of his death, their relationship had long since turned sour. Freddie had apparently learned his lesson from his first two marriages. They had no children, and her pre-nuptial agreement would have left her with only a small payout in case of divorce. He wondered how much she would get now that he was dead.

"And who is this gentleman?" asked Rose.

"David Lowell."

"Oh yes, the astrologer. I've read about you in the papers. You've been looking into Freddie's murder."

"Mrs. Finger, I'm terribly sorry for your loss."

He extended his hand, which she took briefly.

"And to you as well, uh, Mrs. Finger," he said to the blonde.

"Please, call me Tracy," she said, seductively. "An astrologer, huh? What do you think of Libras?"

"I don't do astrology work at funerals."

"Oh, well, maybe you could do my chart sometime."

"Maybe."

"Didn't I see Vivian here earlier?"

"She went back to her hotel," said Lowell. "I think the stress was too much."

"Without saying hello to her step-mother? That's not like her," said Tracy.

Rose laughed. "Step-mother."

"I'm sure it was an oversight," said Lowell. "I'll be seeing her later and would be happy to bring her a message."

Tracy furrowed her brow as if in deep thought. "Just tell her that "mom" says hello and I hope to see her while she's in town. If there's anything I can do to help you catch his killer, please let me know."

"I may have some questions for both of you." He handed each a business card. "Would it be all right if I called upon you in a day or so?"

"Of course," said Tracy, "I'll do whatever I can to help." She looked over at Rose. "Even if it means airing dirty laundry."

Rose's eyes seemed on fire. "Are you making some sort of accusation, Tracy? You know what *accusation* means, don't you? If you need time to look up any of the words I'm using, please let us know." She turned to Lowell. "You know how hard it can be for blondes."

"I'm just saying that the police should look into *every* possibility, that's all. Just how much will you get now that he's dead?" asked the second Mrs. Finger.

"Not as much as you took him for," said the third.

"Yeah, but more than you would have gotten if he had the chance to throw you out like he was planning."

"You mean like he did to you?"

"At least *I* had children with him. What did you do for him?"

"How about getting him sober and saving his life," said Rose.

"Kidding yourself as always. I thought you were in therapy?"

"Nice to see you again, Tracy." said Rose. "Try not to trip over your tongue." She turned to Lowell. "It was nice meeting you, Mr. Lowell. Please feel free to call me anytime," she looked over at Tracy, "especially if you want to know the truth about things."

"Can *you* think of anyone who might want Freddie dead?" he asked.

"I can't think of many who didn't."

She handed Lowell her card and departed.

Tracy also said her goodbyes and walked off in the opposite direction. She didn't give Lowell anything.

"Well," said Bobby, "what did you think of that?"

Chapter Ten

It was proving difficult to get Tracy's correct birth information. All Lowell knew was that she was a Libra. She had lied about her age so much that every website gave a different year. He somehow doubted she would be more forthright in person.

The second Mrs. Finger lived in a new high rise on West 89th Street. She came to the door dressed in a pink and white chemise and a matching skirt. They were both sheer and quite see-through.

Lowell tried to look at anything but her as they sat in her living room.

"How do you take it?" she asked.

"I beg your pardon?"

"I've made some fresh coffee." She pointed to the table near the couch. "How do you take it?"

"Oh. Milk and sugar, please."

She mixed his beverage and handed it to him.

The apartment was large and furnished with obviously expensive pieces. Ceiling to floor windows let the early sunlight pour in. Although visibly a woman of means with several staff, a sense of disarray was on display. Papers were scattered around, magazines lay open on tables, and there were a few articles of clothing strewn around. Evidence of her children was also present everywhere. Toys and coloring books lay on the floor.

"I suppose you want to know what that was all about, yesterday."

"Well, I did notice a certain amount of hostility between you two, but I'm really only interested in things that are directly connected to Freddie's murder."

She sipped her coffee. "Isn't this a beautiful view? I paid almost a million more to have the southern exposure." She stood up and walked to the window. "It's such a repressive city without a good view, don't you think?"

She turned toward Lowell and smiled. The outline of her body was quite visible with the morning light behind her.

He cleared his throat and looked down at his coffee. "Tell me about your disagreement with Rose."

"That woman is a little gold digger. She was nothing but a two-bit actress who couldn't get a real gig so she set her sights on Freddie, hoping to cash in. But he was too smart for her and made her sign a pre-nup."

"I assume you didn't have such an arrangement with Freddie?"

"No, we were in love and trusted each other."

"That didn't work out too badly for you, did it?"

"I was with him for ten years. I put up with his cheating and his drugs and all the rest of it. I got just what I deserved in our settlement, nothing more."

"So why is there such animosity between you and Rose?"

"She's the little bitch that stole my husband. Did you know they were involved while I was still married to him? He met her in LA while they were on tour. From what I heard she stalked him for weeks until he finally gave in."

"That must have made you mad."

"You bet it did. I could have killed them!"

She paced back and forth in front of the window.

"Hey," she said suddenly, "I didn't mean I would actually kill him. I didn't do it! I think *she* did it."

She sat on the couch next to him, her leg touching his. "Don't you see? She wouldn't get anything if he divorced her. Maybe a million and change. This way she can contest any will he made up and throw the pre-nup out the window. She did it, you can count on that. Maybe I could help you in your investigations?" she purred.

The intercom rang.

"Damn." She got up from the couch, walked over to the house phone and picked it up. "Yes, what is it? Oh crap, I remember. Let me change and I'll be right down."

She hung up and turned toward Lowell. "I'm sorry, I promised to chair a fundraiser this afternoon and they've come to pick me up. Perhaps we could get together later and compare notes?"

"Perhaps. I need your birth information. I'm having a bit of trouble finding it."

"I was born October 21st."

"And the year?"

"Oh, a lady never tells her age." She walked him to the door.

◇◇◇

The third Mrs. Finger lived on West 10th Street in a townhouse she'd owned jointly with Freddie.

Dressed in a conservative black pant suit with a ruffled shirt and black flats, she was the antithesis of Tracy.

"Please come in."

Lowell entered the townhouse. The first thing he noticed was the meticulous order with which everything had been arranged. There wasn't a crooked picture, a magazine out of place, or anything that could hint at disorganization.

They sat on matching chairs in the living room. A maid came in and brought coffee and tiny cup cakes. He ate one and sipped the coffee.

"You spoke to Tracy, I assume."

"Yes, I was at her place this morning."

Rose took a sip of coffee. "Did she wear any clothes?"

"Barely."

"That's what I thought. What did she tell you, that I stole Freddie away from her?"

"Something like that."

"Nothing could be further from the truth. They were finished long before I came into the picture. You saw the way she dressed. Their marriage didn't have a chance from the beginning."

"Why is that?"

"Between Freddie's whoring and her trampy ways it was tempestuous from the very start."

"Your marriage wasn't?"

Rose was concise in everything she did. There wasn't a movement out of place or a wasted moment. She moved one of the cupcakes from the edge of the plate to the center creating a more symmetrical design. Her birth information was not in question. Every mention of her gave the same date. She was a Virgo, born September 10th, 1977 about nine-twenty in the morning. She had a Moon–Venus conjunct in Leo in sextile to Pluto, and an early Scorpio rising sign. Her sexuality bubbled just under the surface.

"I had no illusions about Freddie. When I married him I never expected to have children and I wasn't in it for the pension. I hoped we could have fun for a few years and that maybe it would help my career."

"You're not the jealous type?"

She laughed. "If you want to marry a rocker you can't be, unless you want to make yourself crazy."

"Like Tracy?"

"Bingo. She expected Freddie to be a husband. He wasn't capable of it."

"His cheating bothered her?"

"Certainly it did."

"But you say she was promiscuous as well."

"So? Haven't you ever known someone who demanded faithfulness while out whoring around? That's what Tracy was like, still is, I assume. She's a spoiled little princess who expects men to lose their minds once she drops her drawers."

"Freddie didn't lose his mind?"

"Freddie didn't give a damn about any one woman. Since he was a child he had always attracted females."

They sipped their coffee in silence for a moment.

"But you could inherit much more than what your prenuptial agreement states."

"I could, if I planned to sue. But I don't. I get several million dollars, this townhouse, and a home outside of LA. I have quite a bit stashed away from our years together, and that's more than enough for me."

"You're not planning to contest the will?"

"If you think I'm going to spend my time fighting Tracy and all the other cockroaches that are about to come out of the woodwork to lay a claim on Freddie's money, you're crazier than she is."

"So why would Tracy give me the impression that you are in it for the money?"

"Because it's the only way she can compete with me. Freddie left her because of who she is, not because of me or any other woman. All Tracy cares about is money and status. If she believes that I really don't care about these things then she has lost the high moral ground, and she looks like the money-grubbing whore that she is."

Chapter Eleven

It was time to compare notes, so Lowell paid a visit to Lieutenant Roland. He found the cop sitting at his overcrowded desk, coffee cup in hand, looking through a file. Framed pictures of Ronald Reagan and George H. W. Bush hung on the wall behind him. When Lowell came in Roland closed the file and gestured toward the vacant seat.

"What have you got for us?"

Lowell sat. "I'm following a couple of leads. First, I need the answers to a few questions."

"All right, if I can."

"Who owns the townhouse where Freddie was found?"

Roland took a sip of his coffee. "It's owned by a company called Ridgewood Holding in the Cayman Islands. The company recently went belly up and they're trying to dump the property. There are several bids on the place, all of them legitimate."

"Can I have a list of the bidders on the property, as well as any bidders who recently dropped out?"

"Sure, if you've got the time to sift through it all I'd be delighted for any information you come up with."

Lowell pointed to the stack of files on his desk. "Lieutenant, you've got dozens of unsolved cases. I've got one case, at the moment. Obviously I'm going to be able to concentrate better on this case than you can. I'll be happy to share my knowledge."

"I've got a theory of my own that seems to hold water."

"Oh?"

"Well, all evidence points to Freddie's murder being one of opportunity," said the policeman.

"What do you mean?"

"Freddie was probably killed by someone who had a grudge against him, a boyfriend or husband."

"Or maybe an ex-wife or widow?" said Lowell.

"Ah, I see you've met two of the Mrs. Fingers. Are you looking into their activities?"

"They are in the active file. Although I doubt that either of them could have done this alone."

"It wouldn't be the first time a wife got help disposing of an unwanted husband, or ex."

"I'll follow up on it."

"The way I see it," continued Roland, "someone else killed Gene and Wally, maybe two different people for two completely different reasons. Remember, at first we weren't even sure if Gene had been murdered at all or if it was an accident. Someone saw an opportunity to get back at Freddie for some sexual misconduct, and figured this would be a good time to kill him and throw us off the track, making us think it was related to the others. And it worked, for a while."

"And you feel this way, why?"

"Well, except for the fact that they are all rock stars, and that they were all killed in New York City, these three have nothing in common. They weren't personal friends, they didn't see the same shrink, and even their music was totally different. Gene sang ballads, Wally spewed rage, and Freddie was a head-banger rocker."

Lowell nodded. "Go on."

"In each case the modus operandi was unique. The weapon used was different each time. Gene was pushed out a window, Wally was stabbed, and Freddie was shot. No, these murders were not related, I'd bet my reputation on it. In fact, with the public screaming for some resolution I may go public with my ideas later today."

Lowell sighed. "Listen, Lieutenant, I wouldn't do that so fast if I were you. I'm not sure these murders weren't all committed by the same person or persons. These crimes are an extension of a financial matter, of that I'm certain. And they are all connected. You may be right about there being an emotional element involved, especially in Freddie's case, but why don't you give me a few days before you go public with anything?"

"I've got to do something soon. Some music acts are threatening to cancel their New York dates. Everyone is afraid to go out on stage. They think someone is waiting to pop 'em off the first chance they get. And when you're playing in front of twenty thousand people, it's hard to keep an eye on everyone."

"Maybe it *would* be better if they weren't so exposed, at least until we solve this thing."

"Do you know how much money rock shows generate in this city? How much a tour by one of these groups earns? And not just for the band. There are t-shirts, concession stands, record sales, taxi drivers, restaurants, hotels. The list goes on and on. The mayor called me yesterday, personally. And this time you're way off base."

"Are you willing to risk that? Just give me more time to look into some things and I promise I'll tell you everything I learn. You can even take credit when we solve this thing, okay?"

"Well," Roland cleared his throat, "I suppose I can stall things for a day or two. But this has to be solved, and soon. It's my ass on the line."

"But lieutenant, I'm not sure we're going to be able to solve this in a day or two. The planetary aspects show a continuing unfolding situation that will not be resolved for a while."

"Why not?"

"Mercury is in retrograde and you probably won't get your solution until it goes direct. That is when the secrets will come out. I doubt that you will know who your killer is until then. If you go off half cocked and arrest the wrong person on this retrograde you will regret it."

"I can't wait two more weeks, they'll have my head. Can't you do something?"

Lowell laughed. "Well, we could give Mercury a great big push and turn it around."

"Just do what you can. And I'm not waiting for your damned planets to line up."

"Let me know if you find a way around them. In the meantime we must continue to investigate."

Chapter Twelve

Lowell sat at his desk punching up chart after chart. He knew Roland was wrong. While there were undertones of this being a crime of passion, the real motivation was greed. Freddie's murder had to do with money, of that he was sure, in fact, all the deaths did, even though, according to everyone he'd spoken to, there were no financial problems.

Wally and Freddie's death charts still showed a similar energy, while Gene's was quite different. This distinction bothered Lowell, and he set out to clarify the issue.

He called Boston and spoke to Gene's manager, Richard Frey. Gene's finances were, if anything, in better shape than Freddie's. He had married about five years ago, giving his wife control of the family fortune. At his death, Gene was worth at least several hundred million dollars, there were no law suits pending, no paternity accusation, nothing.

Redfish's manager, Johnny Gleason, wasn't so forthright. Although he was based in New York he refused to see Lowell in person. They spoke briefly on the phone. At first he wouldn't discuss Wally's finances. But when Lowell explained that the alternative was to have the DA order a complete and thorough investigation of all the financial records for the last ten years, he became chatty. But here too, there was nothing but positive financial news and money was not an issue.

After speaking to the three managers Lowell found their attitudes virtually interchangeable. They each expressed superficial grief over the death of their client, yet all were busier than they had ever been, promoting the death of a rock star.

Mort had dug out the birth information for the three managers. Even though it would eventually cost each of them a fortune with the death of their stars, nobody was beyond suspicion.

Their birth information was easy to acquire over the Internet. James Gleason, Redfish's manager, was born November 30th, 1949, at 7:27 p.m. in Detroit. Robert Frey, Gene's manager, was born December 29th, 1948, at 3:14 p.m. in Boston.

Larry Latner was born October 12, 1949, at 6:55 a.m. in the Bronx. This gave him a 12th House Libra Sun conjunct Neptune, not a very strong aspect, although with the Sun ruling his 10th House of career, and Neptune ruling the music business it made sense that he would choose this profession. But he did have Mars conjunct Pluto in the 10th House, which showed a ruthless, unyielding side to his personality, especially in his career pursuits. But whether that was powerful enough to overcome the weakness of that Neptune placement to commit murder was the question. Lowell didn't think so.

None of the managers' charts showed a particularly violent nature. But, as Lowell had learned through the years, that did not mean that they weren't capable of murder, given the right incentive. But what would be their motivation to kill the golden goose?

He walked over to the window. The view from his office was a dazzling look uptown, with the Empire State Building still clear through the summer haze.

◇◇◇

Sarah looked up from her typing when the front door opened and a gawky man entered, his limbs seemingly disconnected from the rest of his body. Sarah couldn't help but think of the do-da man from the old R. Crumb comics her father used to read after smoking pot in the basement when he thought Sarah and her brother were asleep.

"Hi, doll, you miss me?"

"Well, look who the wind blew in. Hi, Mort. How was Florida?"

Mort wasn't tall, but his limbs seemed exceptionally long, which gave the illusion of height. He had been locally well-known as a psychic long before Lowell hired him. He came to work at the Starlight Detective Agency about five years before.

"A little family problem, but nothing too serious. You look as lovely as ever." He furrowed his brow in a most unnatural looking way. "What is it? What's bothering you?"

"Nothing, don't be silly."

"Oh, Sarah, you know you can't hide stuff from me. I can tell that you're worried about your boyfriend, aren't you?"

She nodded.

"You two had another fight?"

She nodded again. "I'm afraid he's going to leave me."

"Don't worry. This will resolve itself soon. Although, if you don't mind my saying, it would be better for you if he did."

"Really?" Sarah's face lit up. "Things will get better?"

"Yes, very soon."

"The boss told me the same thing."

"Well, when we both come to the same conclusion it's usually correct. And how are things here?"

"If I told you, you wouldn't believe me. You'll never guess who's been coming around."

"I assume from your reaction it's someone important. And since the boss was working on Freddie Finger's murder, um, I guess a few rock stars. Hmm, maybe New Yorkers. Could it be…?"

"Oh stop that," interrupted Sarah. "At least let me try and surprise you." She filled him in on the events of the past few days. He was very disappointed at missing a chance to meet some of his heroes, but took it stoically.

"Let's get some lunch," he said, once Sarah had brought him up to date.

"Alright, I'll see if the boss wants anything."

Sarah buzzed him.

He picked up the intercom phone. "What's up?"

"Mort's here and I'm going out to get lunch. Do you want something?"

"Get me an avocado and Swiss on rye and some potato salad. And ask Mort to come in."

"Okay, I'll be right back."

She picked up her purse and started for the door.

"I was thinking of going to the track tonight with my girl-friends," she said. "Uh, what do you think? Will I win?"

Mort squished his face into a most peculiar frown. "The track, huh? Odd place. Still, let me think. Look for the number five. It should be a long shot, a big one."

"Thanks, Mort!"

"I also see a woman dressed in bright colors, maybe flowers. She has red hair just like yours and her name begins with a D or a B. She works in a business that can help you in some way. And remember, number five is very important."

She headed out the door.

Mort entered Lowell's office. "How are ya?"

"Mort, how was your trip? Is the family okay?"

"Nothing too tragic."

"Good." Lowell handed him a slip of paper. "First thing I want you to do is to find out who owns this holding company in the Cayman Islands, who these potential bidders on the property are, including the two that dropped their bids. Then I want you to find someone named Marty Winebeck, a musician about sixty, whose last known address was somewhere in New York City."

Mort was one of the best hackers in the world. He was asked to leave MIT after he used their computer to penetrate secret government files. It would have been too embarrassing to prosecute him, so the government offered him a job in their computer section, which he turned down. He was also a psychic, could read the emotions of many people he sat near, even their actual thoughts at times, something that could amaze, or unnerve. For some reason he was unable to read Lowell's thoughts, and once the astrologer was sure of this, he hired him. Besides, as a scientist, which is how Lowell saw himself and his astrological work, he was not about to rely on any unsubstantiated concept, plan, or prediction. It simply wasn't in his nature.

But truth be told, he had been quite impressed and amazed by the man on more than one occasion.

The first time Lowell saw his chart he recognized that the same wiring that gave Mort his unusual psychic abilities also allowed him to see things in a unique non-linear fashion. His intuition was remarkable, and he was thus able to associate things that others didn't. This helped him travel through the web more quickly than most people. It was on the Internet that he served his most useful purpose for the firm.

◇◇◇

Mort went to his office and got to work. In less than an hour he had bypassed the security of the Ridgewood Holding Company based in the Caymans, as well as Morton Realtors, the New York-based agents for the sale. He printed out the pertinent information and walked into Lowell's office.

"Morton Realty has been around for decades. They seem to be on the up and up. But I can't find anything on Ridgewood Holding."

"I want you to follow up on this. I want to know who Ridgewood is. Use that rather peculiar brain of yours and dig it out."

"Okay, but this one isn't going to be easy."

"I know. The Cayman's don't require much in the way of proof or paper trails, which is why they are so popular."

"And here is a list of bidders on the property, including the two who dropped out." Mort handed a few sheets of paper to Lowell.

"You know what I want now?"

"Yeah," eagerness in his voice, "you want me to track all these people down on the Internet, invade their privacy, and break about a dozen laws to find out everything I can about them."

"Right," Lowell returned his attention back to his computer.

Mort frowned, thought for a moment. "Okay." He went back to his office.

"And find me Marty Winebeck!" Lowell shouted.

About an hour later Mort walked in and handed Lowell a piece of paper with a list of all the participants involved in the 80th Street house.

"Okay," said Lowell, "good work. Anything special here?"

"Nope, it all checks out. The bidders all seem legitimate."

"All right, anything on Marty Winebeck?"

"That guy isn't easy to find. He's got no driver's license, he's not affiliated with any group, and he's never been on a jury."

"Well, keep trying."

"I have an idea. He's a musician, right?"

Lowell nodded.

"Broke, I assume?"

A shrug and a nod.

"Uh huh, give me another hour, I'll find him."

True to his word, about fifty minutes later he handed Lowell another piece of paper from the department of housing with information regarding a tenant – landlord dispute.

"How'd you find him?"

Mort's head bobbed up and down. "First in the housing court files. That's one of the easiest to get into, they know nothing about security, and most of the stuff is public access anyway. I figured he's a musician, so he's bound to have had troubles with the landlords through the years. I only hoped it was within the last seven years. They expunge the files and move them to storage, tougher to get into. He was evicted from a place on 54th Street about six years ago. I was able to get his info from that court proceeding, but then he disappeared again."

"So you don't have him?"

Mort smiled. "Sure I do."

"How?"

"Everybody's got cable," his smile broadened, as he handed Lowell the second piece of paper with Marty Winebeck's information, including his social security number, present address, and a history of his tax returns. "Once I had his present address and social security number everything else was easy."

Lowell put the other piece of paper into a folder and scrutinized this page.

"The poor bastard," he said, as he read the amount of income Marty had declared though the years. "The best time was in the early nineties when he had several years of $40,000 a year or more in reported income, just enough to survive in the city. Other years ranged from $16,000 to about $25,000. How he survived is a mystery." He read the address. "Probably a walk-up, rent-stabilized, one room apartment."

Lowell took the birth information, punched up the natal chart and scrutinized it for a few minutes. "Marty was born March 6, 1950, at 6:13 a.m. He's a Pisces with the Sun in the 1st House opposite Saturn, both in square to the mid-heaven. This is a difficult chart that shows struggle and conflict. Nothing comes easy to this guy. If he makes it at all, it will be late in life. With Chiron on the mid-heaven it was a rough career path that implied a lot of sacrifice. Mercury is conjunct Jupiter in Aquarius, so he is very bright. But they are buried in the 12th House, and it may be hard for him to express himself except through the arts. The Moon in Libra is conjunct Neptune, once again showing how prominent Neptune is for people in the music business."

He got up and stretched. "I think it's time to look in on Mr. Winebeck."

"Aren't you going to call him first?"

"I think a more impromptu visit is warranted."

"What if he's not home?"

"How do you feel about a little breaking and entering?"

Chapter Thirteen

It would have been too conspicuous to have Andy drive them in the limo, so they hailed a cab and had him drop them two blocks from Marty's apartment.

"Are cabs getting smaller or am I getting larger," Mort grumbled, as they got out on 88th Street and York Avenue.

The neighborhood was very quiet. A few people were walking their dogs, and a well-dressed couple came out of the York Grill and hurried passed. They walked up York Avenue past Conti's deli on the corner and turned down 89th Street to Marty's building.

Lowell pushed the buzzer. There was no answer. He pushed again, and still, nothing. He looked up and down the street and then gave Mort a nod.

The strange man took out a small zippered case and opened it, revealing all sorts of tiny instruments. He removed one and bent down to work on the front door lock. In about ten seconds they were inside. There was an inner door as well, but this one wasn't even locked.

It was a pre-war building as unadorned as any they had ever seen. The vestibule was a tiny space with mail boxes on both sides. The walls and ceilings were all painted white. The stairs had brown rubber nailed on top of brown wood.

They bounded up the stairs. Lowell knocked on the door several times, and then nodded once again to Mort. This lock took almost twenty seconds to pick.

"You're slowing down," said Lowell.

Mort snorted. "Guaranteed burglar proof." He pointed to the lock.

"Obviously."

"If you don't mind," Mort said as he put his hand on the front door, "I'll wait outside."

"That would be best. Buzz twice if you see anyone coming in the building."

Lowell entered the tiny apartment quietly. One room, as he had predicted. There wasn't much to it, a futon bed that doubled as a couch, a coffee table, two chairs, a small computer desk, a dresser, some music equipment, and the joke of a tiny half-kitchen that many New Yorkers were forced to live with.

He began by opening the cabinets above the sink. There was a cheap set of dishes and glasses, two large bowls, four small ones, and one serving tray. The one drawer in the kitchen area contained mismatched forks, spoons, and knives. He moved on to the desk, looking through envelopes and papers. There were a few letters, some junk mail, and a lot of bills. He opened the Con Ed envelope and a disconnect notice fell out. He picked it up and read it: $285.46 was due in three days. He put it back the way he had found it.

He walked around the tiny room taking in everything he saw. *The musical equipment is probably worth more than everything else this guy owns,* he thought. There were some pages that looked like lyrics spewed around the place, a few periodicals, and a copy of a week old *New York Post*, the front page missing. A few pieces of clothing were thrown over one of the chairs, and a pair of old sneakers sat on the floor. The closet held several dress shirts on hangers, one sport jacket, and a well-worn tuxedo.

He sat down on the futon and opened the drawer in the coffee table. He removed the scrapbook and opened it. His eyes grew wide with excitement. Page one was Gene's *New York Post* headline as big as life. Then the second page, there was Wally, with all the sordid details. And finally page three, "Freddy Gets

Fingered." He took out a small digital camera and photographed each page.

He walked over to the computer table and fumbled through the papers scattered on top. The usual emails, advertisements, bills, and scraps littered the desk and the floor near by. He reached into the printer tray and took out a single page. He looked at it. It was a copy of an email Marty had sent a few days before. It said: "Three down and one to go."

Just then the buzzer sounded twice. He folded the paper and put it in his pocket, knowing he was taking a chance removing it, went back to the coffee table and closed the book, careful to put it back exactly as it had been. He quickly looked around to make sure he hadn't noticeably disturbed anything, and then went out the front door. Between the third and second floors he passed a youngish looking though middle-aged man with shoulder length hair. Lowell tried to turn his face away so the man wouldn't recognize him if they met again. He didn't seem to take any interest in Lowell whatsoever.

When he got outside Mort grabbed his arm. "That was him, you know."

"I assumed so."

"Did he see you?"

"I don't think he was paying much attention."

"No," said Mort, knowingly, "he was too worried about money to notice anything."

"I don't doubt it."

They grabbed a cab and returned to the office.

"Top priority," Lowell said, as he sat at his desk. "I want to know everything about Marty Winebeck, and I mean everything. Can you hack into his PC and get to his email?"

"It depends on which server he uses, but most likely I can."

Lowell turned back to his own computer. "Well, do so. And I want you to find out what you can about the eight people this email was sent to."

Chapter Fourteen

"I understand you went to the Meadowlands last night."

Lowell took the coffee cup from Sarah.

"Yeah, the girls wanted to try our luck, and, well, Mort told me I might win. He said to look for the number five, and that I could hit a big one."

"So how did you make out?"

"Oh, you know, okay I guess. We had a good time, that's all that matters."

"Did you win *any* races?"

"Well, no, not exactly. But one of my horses was scratched so I got my two dollars back."

"No number fives?"

"Un uh."

"Sorry."

"Oh, that's all right. I don't blame Mort. It was my decision to go."

"I understand."

"But," she said, "it's weird."

"What is?"

"He also told me that I would meet a redhead whose name begins with a B or a D, and that she could help me in some way."

"And…"

"As we were getting ready to leave I met a woman in a flow-ered dress with red hair, just like mine. Her name was Barbara and she's an agent for commercials on TV. We started to talk and she said I had *a look*, and to call her."

"That part of Mort's prediction was right on the money."

"Speaking of money, how come he can get that right and can't pick a god damned horse? Not a single number five came up all night."

"Karma," replied the astrologer.

She took a handful of losing tickets from her purse and began to tear them up one by one. "You know what you can do with your karma, don't you?"

"You have her card?"

She reached back into her purse and pulled out a business card. "Right here. It has her name, the name of the agency, her email and her phone number. Two one two, eight seven four, five, five, five…" she stopped and looked up at Lowell. "…five."

"I'd call her, if I were you."

◇◇◇

Lowell was alone when the phone rang. Sarah was out getting lunch and he thought about ignoring it, as he often did when she was away from her desk. He hated dealing with the public, and screening his calls was one of Sarah's most important jobs. But on the fourth ring curiosity got the better of him and he picked up the receiver.

"Starlight Detective Agency."

"If you want to know who killed those rockers come to 312 Summer Street in Soho at eight o'clock sharp tonight. And bring that Younger dame with you or the deal is off." The voice was muffled.

"Who are you?"

"Just be there on time."

"What if she doesn't want to come?"

"What?"

"What if Ms. Younger chooses not to accompany me?"

"Are you crazy? Just bring her. And don't be late."

"I'll try. What was that address again?"

There was an exasperated sigh at the other end. "312 Summer Street. Now stop screwing with me."

Sarah came in a few seconds after he'd hung up and saw the look on her boss' face. "What's going on?"

"Rewind the tape to the last call."

She went to her desk and opened the top right hand drawer. Inside was a taping device that was attached to the office phone line. It automatically recorded every call that came in. She rewound the tape. Together they sat and listened to the exchange.

"I kept him on the phone as long as I could. Hoped to recognize the voice or hear something in the background," he said, after they'd heard it several times, "but I can't."

"You're not going, are you?"

"Of course I am."

"Are you crazy? I'm not ready to look for another job at the moment."

"You're sure it's a trap?"

"Aren't you?"

He grinned. "Sure. Why else would I be going?"

"Well, you're certainly not going to endanger Vivian Younger," Sarah said, defiantly.

"No, I wouldn't do that."

"Thank god you have some common sense left."

He was looking at her in a strange way.

"What?"

"Huh? Oh nothing. How tall are you?"

Sarah looked at him askew. "I'm five seven, why?"

"Um hmm, and let's see. Maybe a hat, or a scarf?"

"Oh no, no you don't. I'm not going to be your dummy."

"Now, Sarah, would I ever put you at risk?"

"No sir, my mother only raised one fool, and she lives in Jersey."

"Sarah…"

"No!"

"I'll pay you extra."

"Not a chance in…how much?"

"Five hundred dollars."

"A thousand. And you better not get me shot."

"All right, a thousand."

"Up front."

"Sarah, don't you trust me?"

"Are you kidding? I'm going out and spending it today. I've had my eyes on a pair of seven-hundred dollar shoes for months. If I get bumped off tonight I'm sure not getting screwed out of my good time, too."

"Seven-hundred dollar shoes? What are they made of?"

"It's the stuff that dreams are made of."

"That's got to be the worst Bogie I've ever heard."

She giggled. "Maybe so, but it's the stuff that *my* dreams are made of."

Sarah had a closet full of shoes that she fawned over.

He took the money from the wall safe and paid her in cash. She immediately went downtown to 8th Street and bought her shoes.

To Lowell they were just that, shoes. But to Sarah and every woman she could think of to call and tell about them, they were apparently something else, something with the ability to make women, including Sarah's mother, envious.

<><><>

Sarah's disguise had to be convincing enough from a distance. Lowell had no intentions of letting her get any closer than was necessary. They picked up a blond wig, a paisley scarf, and large sunglasses.

She put on her outfit in Lowell's dressing room and looked at herself in the mirror. "I wouldn't be fooled for a minute."

She came out of the dressing room and presented herself to Lowell.

He looked down at her feet, blue pumps. "No good. Sneakers."

"What? They won't go with what I have on."

"So wear blue sneakers. Sorry to ruin your ensemble, but I insist."

Andy was waiting when they walked out of the building at seven-thirty.

"Andy, take the drive south and get off at Houston and head west. I'll tell you where to drop us when we're downtown."

"Okay, boss."

They got on the FDR Drive at 79th Street. *What a strange city*, he thought. *This antiquated roadway was obsolete the day they opened it in the 1930s. Today it can't carry half the load expected during rush hour. They continue to expand the city, yet they spend virtually nothing on the infrastructure. How long before the wear and tear in the underbelly of this city causes it to all fall apart?*

The city flew by, uptown became midtown, which morphed into downtown. They got off the drive and headed west on Houston. When they got to First Avenue the detective said, "Stop here, Andy. Stay nearby."

Lowell and Sarah exited the limo and waited until it drove away.

"Why did you have him drop us here instead of at the address?"

"One should always approach an unsure situation carefully."

"You do have a gun, don't you?"

"Gun? No, I don't like the nasty little things."

She stared at him, wondering if she'd ever get to wear her new shoes.

They walked a few blocks west on Houston. At Broadway there was a large fruit stand. Lowell picked up a few melons, squeezing each, and finally chose a large, green, rather unripe looking honeydew.

"What are you doing picking fruit out? Have you lost your mind?"

He ignored her. He next picked out about a dozen small, unappetizing looking nectarines. He had the salesman put the fruit into three bags and then paid him. Sarah grabbed one of the nectarines.

"Couldn't you at least get something we can eat? This thing is as hard as a rock."

He took it back from her and replaced it in the bag. "Just pay attention. We may have to act quickly."

Sarah was not happy. She had no interest in being a hero. Her boss was a good man, he paid her much more than she would make anywhere else, and for that she was thankful. But he was strange, and his clientele was strange, and his friends were strange, and now she was going to get killed in a meeting with a stranger.

They walked another block and then turned right. At the second light they went down a dark side street.

"This is the block," he said, as her grip on his arm grew tighter.

They found the number and he was about to ring the bell when he noticed two men at the end of the street eyeing them. Sarah saw them too.

"Oh my god," she muttered quietly.

The men began to move slowly toward them. She stiffened and began to shake.

He took her hand. "Everything's going to be fine. All I have to do is get close to these guys and explain things. They'll understand."

"Understand? They're going to chop us up".

By now the men had moved closer. Lowell took her and placed her in the deep recess of the doorway.

"Stay here," he implored, "no matter what you think is going on, wait here. Just trust me."

He walked down the three steps to the street and approached them, stopping about five feet away. One was short, maybe five seven, but had a mean look that more than compensated for his stature. The other was a giant of a man, about six five, with dark brown hair and a scar across the left side of his face.

"Do we have a problem here?" He didn't recognize either of them.

"No, *we* don't have a problem buster, you do." The little guy pulled a gun from his jacket and aimed it at the astrologer, just as Lowell swung his right arm in a wide arc. The bag containing the unripe melon left his hand. It hit the man on the left side of his head with enough force to knock him to the ground. His skull cracked on the cement.

The big man reached his gigantic hands toward Lowell who threw the two remaining bags of fruit into the man's face. He was off balance as he put his hands up for protection, allowing Lowell to sweep his feet out from underneath him, causing him to tumble to the ground. He tried to stand, but before he could get his footing, Lowell took hold of the man's wrist with one hand and placed the other on his elbow, and turned his body to the left, twisting the arm violently. The man fell back to the ground writhing in pain.

Sarah came down the steps and they hurried past the wounded men and down the sidewalk toward the better lit and more populated avenue. Sarah was happy that she was wearing sneakers.

A blue sports car that had been parked down the street had come to life.

As Lowell and Sarah got to the end of the street and were crossing to the other side, the driver suddenly revved his engine and appeared not to have any desire to stop at the light. Or at them.

Lowell pulled Sarah back just as Lowell's limo drove into the crosswalk from the avenue. The blue car swerved violently and slammed into a fire hydrant on the curb. The air bag deployed, and water bubbled up through the car's engine, now parked firmly on top of the hydrant.

Andy hopped out of the limo. "Are you two okay?" He pulled the back door open and Lowell and Sarah dove in. Then he got behind the wheel. "Boss?"

"I think we should get out of here. Who knows if there are more of them? Call Lieutenant Roland and tell him what happened."

"That was one of the most amazing things I've ever seen," Sarah said, once they were secure in the limousine. "Where did you learn to fight like that? And what was that thing with the fruit? I mean, where the hell does someone learn tricks like that?"

Lowell took a deep gulp of cold water from a bottle from the fridge and slowed his breath. "You know I've studied aikido for many years. I've mentioned it before. It was a combination of that and common sense. I was greatly influenced by a book I read in the eighties called *Shibumi*, written by Rodney William Whitaker, under the name Trevanian." he replied. "You should read it someday."

"What's it about?"

"It's about many things, including finding one's proper path in life, and learning to use what's available to you at any given time on that path to make a situation work out best." He wiped the condensation from the bottle onto a napkin. "And it helps to have back-up like Andy."

Chapter Fifteen

Roland paced angrily in his office.

"It thought we had a deal. We were going to keep the other informed of what was going on. Then I find out you put your life at risk running around last night playing Batman. Why didn't you call me before you went downtown?"

"They wouldn't have shown themselves if you had come," replied Lowell.

"They showed themselves all right, and almost knocked you out of commission. And it's bad enough that you put yourself in harm's way. But you took poor Ms. Palmer here and risked her safety as well."

Sarah was sitting on a chair, her legs pulled up under her, looking very stylish in her new seven-hundred dollar shoes.

"Oh Lieutenant, I was so scared I didn't know what to do," she said, in a little girl voice.

Lowell shot her a quick scowl.

"You might want to consider different employment."

"I have, Lieutenant." She stroked her shoes. "Believe me, I have."

"Can we get to the important issues here?" Lowell re-knotted his ponytail, which he did whenever he was perturbed. "What did you get on the men who attacked us?"

"Nothing. They were all gone by the time you bothered to call us and we could get someone down there."

"What about the car?"

"Stolen. Just what you'd expect. It was a dangerous thing to do, and you didn't get anything out of it."

"Quite the contrary. I now know that I'm on the right track. I've stirred up the hornet's nest, and now it's a question of locating it. One of the leads we're following is the right one, otherwise they wouldn't have taken a run at us. So let's see what we've got."

"Okay," said Roland, "what about this Winebeck character?"

"His chart does show that he has a temper, and he's overly emotional, but then he is a musician. His Mars Uranus opposition could make him react violently at times, but it takes a lot to plan and carry out such a gruesome attack. Also, I don't know if there's really a motive."

"You said he and Freddie had a fight?"

"That was over twenty years ago."

"I've seen people hold a grudge for longer than that. What happened?"

"Well, Freddie threw him off a stage in Buffalo and broke the guy's leg. Then Freddie ostensibly had him blackballed so he couldn't get work in the music business for many years."

"Yeah, you're right," said the Lieutenant, snidely, "just because a guy breaks your leg and ruins your career you don't think that's a good enough reason to kill him. What exactly would be a motive in your mind?"

"This isn't the way someone would go about doing it if he was holding in his anger all these years. He might wait until Freddie was alone and pop him. And what about the other two murders? How do they fit in?"

"I told you, the other two have nothing to do with Freddie. I'm going to concentrate on this killing and once we get the murderer you'll see I was right. What else you got on this Winebeck guy?"

As difficult as it was going to be to explain how he came into possession of them without admitting his own legal circumvention, Lowell reluctantly gave the email and the photographs of the bizarre scrapbook to the policeman.

The Lieutenant looked at the photos, read the email, and then whistled. "This is enough for me." He hit the intercom and screamed: "Murphy, get in here."

A moment later a tall, sandy-haired man entered. "Yes sir?"

"I want you to go to this address and pick up one Marty Winebeck for questioning."

"If he doesn't want to come?"

"Well, just see to it that he does."

"Lieutenant, I really think you're jumping the gun here," said Lowell. "All you've got is circumstantial evidence. That email could be about anything."

"Yeah, and these pictures could be from his vacation to the Grand Canyon, but they're not. Look, I won't ask you how you got this, and I don't want you to tell me, but let's stop bullshitting each other and bring this bozo in to answer some questions, all right? Are you in possession of this macabre memorabilia?"

Lowell shook his head.

"Then I think it's time for a search warrant."

He picked up the phone and called the DA's office, explained the situation and requested the warrant be issued. Due to the high profile of the case, this was carried out expeditiously. He handed the warrant to Murphy and sent him, along with two uniforms, to pick up Marty.

"I think you're wrong, Lieutenant. This guy hasn't got the resources to do this."

"Yeah and what about the other eight guys he sent that email to?"

"Mort is checking them out. They are all musicians in their fifties or sixties."

"You think between them nine guys could pull this off?"

Lowell had to admit the possibility. "I suppose so."

Chapter Sixteen

Marty walked into the kitchen and sat at the table. The apartment's only two windows faced northeast, giving him a partial view of the East River. This was such a peaceful neighborhood. Sometimes in the morning he would take his coffee and sit on the stoop at 1700 York with a few of his neighbors just to chat. Asphalt Green, once an actual asphalt plant now transformed into a recreation center, was one block north and he'd often go there and watch the kids and their parents come to this quiet oasis in an otherwise loud and hectic city.

He took a container of yogurt from the fridge and grabbed a spoon from the mismatched set of silverware in a drawer that stuck every time he pushed it closed. He picked up his acoustic guitar and sat on the couch. He began to finger-pick "Freight Train," one of the first songs he ever learned on the guitar using the Travis picking style he'd studied many years before. He meandered around the instrument for a few minutes until an idea came to him, and he began to develop a melody. *It sounds familiar*, he thought, *not too familiar I think*. A great song is one that you think you've heard before. Once it exists it's as if it always did, and you wonder why nobody ever thought of it before. Sometimes someone had. That's what copyright lawyers were for.

His computer beeped. He put the guitar down and walked over to the desk and read the message. It was from Steve Whoo, a drummer he knew. It was in response to the email he had sent.

This one said: "You're either really lucky or a lot meaner than you look."

He laughed. Then he wrote back: "The first two were on your list as well, if I remember correctly. Maybe this one was just to throw us off the track."

He chuckled again, and then pushed send. He printed out Steve's email and his own response and gathered up the papers. He went back to the couch and opened the coffee table drawer. He took out the *death* album and went to the last page, which had two pockets attached, one on either side. He was about to put the emails into the right side pocket when realized there were only two where there should have been three, the two from today and the one he had sent out yesterday. Where was that one? He searched the entire house, not a daunting project, but still could not find it.

He knew he had printed it and was sure he had left it in the printer tray to put away later. This wasn't something he would forget.

He opened the bottom drawer of his dresser and took out a tiny wooden chest. He sat on the couch and opened it, while he pondered the mystery of the missing email. He took out his medicine container and pipe, and poured a bit of the substance into the bowl. He was just about to light it when his buzzer rang. He wasn't expecting anyone, and people rarely popped in. Maybe it was Beth, his girlfriend. But she was on the Cape with her sister and wasn't due back for days. Besides, she had her own key. Well, maybe she came back early and forgot the key.

He hit the intercom button and spoke. "Yes, who is it?"

"Marty Winebeck?"

"Yes, who are you?"

"My name is Sergeant Murphy. NYPD. May we come up?"

What the fuck? "Sure…sorry about the stairs."

He buzzed them up and rushed back to the table, now very glad he hadn't had time to light the pipe. He put it back into the wooden box and placed it all in the coffee table drawer.

A few minutes later there was a knock on the door. Marty opened it and let Sergeant Murphy and two other cops into his apartment.

"What's this all about?" asked Marty.

The Sergeant took a piece of paper from his pocket and said: "Marty Winebeck?"

"You know who I am."

"Marty Winebeck?" repeated the policeman, adhering to protocol.

"Yeah, yeah, I'm him."

"We have a warrant to search your apartment and we wish the pleasure of your company at the 19th precinct."

"A search warrant! What the hell do you expect to find here?"

"We'll let you know when we find it." Murphy waved the two cops past him. Marty watched open-mouthed as they started to open drawers and go through his desk.

"I really object …"

"Nothing to hide, no problem. Mr. Winebeck, are you willing to accompany me to the precinct voluntarily?" asked Murphy.

"Ha, voluntarily, or what? You'll voluntarily toss me down the stairs and into your car?"

"Sir," indignation in the officer's voice, "I am a member of New York finest. If you'd rather not join me now, it'll be necessary for the Lieutenant to issue a warrant for your arrest. Then I'll have to come back here and read you your rights, handcuff you, take you downstairs past your neighbors, drive you to the precinct, process you through the system, which will be on your record…"

"All right, I get it. Sure I'll accompany you."

One of the two uniformed cops came up to Murphy and whispered something to him.

"Yes," said Murphy, aloud, "take the computer and the scrapbook. What else did you find?"

"Well," the cop held up Marty's stash box, "we found this." He opened it and took out the pipe and a small sandwich baggie of pot.

"Take that too. We'll see what the Lieutenant wants to do about it later."

They took Marty down to the street where a patrol car and a plain sedan sat waiting. Murphy gestured for Marty to sit in front.

"You're not under arrest," said Murphy getting into the sedan's diver's seat, "despite the marijuana, so you might as well sit up here with me."

Chapter Seventeen

Marty was placed in a room with a table and three chairs. There was a mirror covering one wall. On the other side of the mirror sat Lowell, Roland, and an assistant DA.

"You go in there first," said Lowell, "and I'll come later."

Roland entered the interrogation room and sat at the desk opposite Marty.

"How you doing?"

"Well, I was sitting quietly in my home about to make myself something to eat, and now I'm sitting in a police station scared to death. How do you think I'm doing?"

"I understand how you feel."

"Good, then I can go home now?"

"Not just yet. First of all, you were found in the possession of a controlled substance."

Marty was more furious than scared. "You clowns wave some trumped up search warrant in my face, rummage through my belongings and come up with about forty dollars worth of pot, and you're threatening me? What ever happened to due process, civil rights, privacy?"

"This is post nine-eleven America, buddy, so don't go screaming your liberal crap at me." He took a deep breath. "We'll discuss the drug charges later. But first, do you mind explaining this to me?" He held up the email and the pictures Lowell had taken of the scrapbook.

The musician took the email from Roland's hand and chuck-led. "So that's where it went. Thank god, I thought I was losing my mind. I assume this has something to do with Freddie's murder? Do you want to know what this is all about?"

"Very much." Roland looked over at the mirror. "And while you're at it, you can tell me about your relationship with Freddie Finger. I understand you two didn't get along."

"That's quite an understatement. You've brought it up, so obviously you know about my history with that twerp."

"You're not exactly helping yourself here."

"What am I going to do, lie about it? You know that asshole broke my leg and collar bone, and made it impossible for me to get a decent gig. What should I tell you, that I forgot all about it? Am I sorry Freddie's dead? Hell no, it should have happened decades ago."

"What about the other two musicians who were killed?"

"Wally was another jerk. The world is no worse off without him. But Gene was a nice guy, a gentleman. And he was a good songwriter, nice ballads, not head-banger crap like the other two."

"So you're sorry that Gene is dead, but not Freddie?" probed the policeman.

"Look, I'm sorry for everybody that's dead, all right?"

"You were going to tell me about this scrapbook and email." Just then the door opened and Lowell entered. "This is David Lowell, a private consultant. He'll be sitting in on the rest of this interview."

"Good," said the musician. "It's easier than shouting through the phony mirror."

Lowell chuckled and sat on the third chair.

"So what about this email?"

Marty began. "All right, I'll tell you. It's really quite an interesting story. It was the late nineties. I was making a decent living, for a musician anyway, playing out in the Hamptons in the summers and here in City the rest of the year. There was a group of ten of us, all long-time players, many I had worked with in bands. None of us was exactly setting the world on fire, but we were all good musicians and could at least make a living. And at any time one or more of us could hit it big with a record.

"I played piano bar on the Upper East Side in places frequented by the Wall Street crowd. I was around for years, and eventually made friends with a few of them. The big story that year was about how low the price of gold had dropped. It got to about two-eighty, or something, I don't know that much about it. Anyway, we all got together one night at J.P.'s on First Avenue with our girlfriends to listen to one of the bands some of our group had put together. Someone had a little blow, and someone else had a little smoke, and after the band finished we all went back to my apartment.

"We started playing a variation on Dead Rock Stars. Each of us took a piece of paper and wrote down the names of the four rockers we thought would die first. What was really funny, turned out none of us had chosen the same four. There were some overlaps, but not as many as you would think, although I think Freddie might have been on a lot of lists. Then again, picking a rock star to die young isn't that difficult. But it was a question of who would go first. As dawn hit and some of the girlfriends wanted to go home we felt there had to be closure to the game, so we all agreed to go downtown that week and buy ten-thousand dollars worth of gold coins each and put them in a safe deposit box. I had just been paid $25,000 for an album I worked on, and believed my career was finally taking off, so I reluctantly agreed to the bet. The key was left with a law firm and none of us could get it without the signatures of all of the survivors of the bet. How many times since I've wished I'd kept that money. Anyway, with fees and whatnot, we paid about three-hundred an ounce with the total for the ten of us coming to a hundred grand. We each got ownership of thirty-three and a third ounces."

Roland whistled. "What's that worth today?"

Lowell did some quick math. "With gold trading around seventeen hundred an ounce it would be a grand total of five-hundred and sixty-six thousand dollars. Give or take."

"And the three murdered musicians just happen to be on your list," said Roland. "It sure seems like a motive to me."

The musician shook his head. "It's just a coincidence."

"The problem is," said Roland, "that I simply don't believe in coincidence".

Lowell pondered Marty's story. If it was a ruse it was easy to check out.

"Who was the fourth?"

"Jesus, do you think I put the whammy on them by putting them on my list? How fucking weird is that?" The musician took a few deep breaths. "The fourth isn't like the others. He didn't drink or smoke cigarettes, didn't chase women or do cocaine for a week at a time. I chose him for a different reason."

"So," said Roland, "who was he?"

"Bobby Ludlum."

Both Roland and Lowell were taken aback.

"Why Bobby Ludlum?" asked Lowell. "He's the cleanest, most all American singer in the country, seems the least likely to die young."

"Ludlum has a compulsion for fast cars. He races professionally and has had several crack ups that could have killed him. Frankly, he should have been the first to go."

"Well," said Roland, "this is how I see it. Someone else killed Gene and Wally and you figured this was your best chance of getting back at Freddie and getting closer to that money. So you killed Freddie and hoped we would think they were all done by the same person."

"Where were you the night of June twenty-ninth?" asked Lowell.

Marty reached into his pocket and took out a small date book. "Here it is. I was playing the piano at El Greco's, a Spanish restaurant on 3rd Avenue, from eight until eleven thirty. Call them up, they'll verify it."

"Freddie was probably killed a little bit after midnight, right in that neighborhood." Roland was tapping a pencil on the table. "You may have had time to do it, or had help from someone."

"Do I need a lawyer? Are going to keep me any longer, or can I go home now?"

Roland waved his hands. "Go on and get out of here. But don't go too far."

"Like I have anyplace to go." He looked down at the pot. "Can I have my stuff back?"

"What do you think?"

Marty got up and walked out the door.

"I'll be back," said Lowell.

"Where are you going?" asked Roland, "I want to compare notes on this."

"Yes, yes, I know. I'll be back later." And he rushed out.

He caught up to Marty at the elevators. "I'm sorry about all this."

"Yeah, that's all right. I just wish they'd give me a ride home. I mean, they were nice enough to drag me out of my house, the least they could do is drag me back again."

"Come on. I'll give you a ride. There's a few things I'd like to ask you."

"You got a car?"

Chapter Eighteen

Fat Jimmy DeAngelo sat on his oversized ass on his oversized lounge chair on the oversized terrace of his Battery Park City apartment. His feet were hurting, as they often did, and he was getting a headache. The skinnier man was talking and talking, and Fat Jimmy was tired of hearing his voice.

He took a sip of peppermint tea. His acid reflux was so bad that he couldn't keep anything else down. He hated skinny people. Truth be told, he hated everybody, but especially skinny people. They could eat and drink whatever they wanted to and their feet didn't hurt all the time. If he had his way he wouldn't have anything to do with anybody, but he needed certain people and tolerated their presence. This little putz was one of them.

He stood up and looked over his terrace wall at the Hudson River. He liked living in Battery Park City. It was like being in a suburb but without a packed commuter train and a stupid yard to maintain. Few people came from uptown to visit, and that suited him just fine.

"You let them go."

"But Uncle Jimmy, they had a limo that smashed into me," said Skinny Jimmy. "What was I supposed to do?"

"You were supposed to scare them off," he sneered, "that's what you were supposed to do. Not get the crap beat out of two guys and crack up a car."

"Well, if you had been there you would have understood."

The fat man took a sip of tea, and then belched loudly. "Damn." He held his stomach as he looked over at his nephew eating a meatball sub. "I sent you to take care of something, and now we've got a bigger problem on our hands."

"Why? They can't track us. The car was stolen and there was nobody to identify."

"And you think this puts us in the clear?"

The skinny one took a big bite of the overstuffed sandwich. Skinny Jimmy weighed in at about two twenty. He was only skinny in comparison to his uncle.

Fat Jimmy watched as a dollop of the sauce dribbled down the other man's chin and landed on his pants. "Here," he handed his nephew a napkin, "wipe your pants."

"Huh?"

"Huh?" mimicked Fat Jimmy. *If I didn't love my sister so much,* he thought, *I never would have hired you, you imbecile.*

Life wasn't fair, he'd known so since he was twelve and started blowing up like a blimp. Before that he was a normal child with the typical New Jersey life. Then he started putting on weight and nothing he did seemed to make any difference at all. If he dieted he gained ten pounds. If he starved himself, something that he did periodically, he ended up in the hospital. He came to feel that doctors were all morons and diet books, clinics, and regimens all fraudulent.

Adolescence was a particularly painful time for him. He always fell in love with the pretty, skinny girls, and when they didn't reciprocate it hurt, causing him to build more walls, only strengthening his need for self-reliance.

Other kids spent their time obsessed with each other, listening to songs about love, sneaking off to deserted spots to explore sex, fending their way through the jungle of the teenage years. But all he saw was the view from the eyes of a fat adolescent with no particularly interesting skills or talents, and an abrasive personality, which grew more so with his increased bulk. He was teased and pitied. He hated the pity most of all. Now, at three hundred and eighty pounds, he had given up on personal relationships and had become obsessed with the accumulation of wealth.

He had spent twenty years trading commodities and building up a massive fortune in cash and favors. He was quite willing to compromise what others thought of as morals. He had no such delusion. The world was a game to be won. If you didn't make a hell of a lot of money, you lost. And ever since he got fat at twelve, Fat Jimmy hadn't lost at anything. He only played games he knew he could win.

He was one of the first tenants of the Roadway complex in Battery Park City. The terrace was the main reason. Almost as big as the living room, it was decorated by one of the top designers in the city, with a large table, a bar, and deck chairs. Exotic plants and flowers rimmed the edge. Six months a year he could barbeque and entertain his business associates and the few friends he allowed himself. Most of the time he just liked to lie under the huge umbrella, watch the markets on TV, and eat.

When his nephew was born, Fat Jimmy was twenty years old and already two hundred fifty pounds. His sister adored Jimmy and named her child after him. As the nephew grew up and the uncle grew fatter the family began calling them Fat Jimmy and Skinny Jimmy. The names stuck. Only the family had the nerve to call him Fat Jimmy to his face, one of the many reasons he avoided family reunions. Sometimes they would call him Uncle Fatty when Skinny Jimmy was around. Fat Jimmy hated it. And he hated his nephew.

"So now what do you want me to do, Uncle Jimmy?"

"Nothing. I'll handle this from now on."

Skinny Jimmy was about to say something. For months he'd wanted to tell off his uncle, but he was scared of the man and could never confront him. "You know…" he began.

His uncle turned and faced him. "Did you have something you wanted to say?"

"I…I…I…"

"Yes, I see, I…I…I…Was that all?" He turned dismissively and continued looking at the river.

He nephew walked back into the apartment. He went into the kitchen, overstuffed, just like everything else in his uncle's life, and took a bottle of Stolichnaya from the freezer. He poured a healthy double into a soda glass and drank it in one shot. He coughed once and then put the bottle back.

"I'll take care of it, you stuffed toad," he said to the refrigerator. Then he walked out the front door.

Fat Jimmy got up from the chair and shuffled his great bulk into the apartment. It was time to shower, a task he didn't look forward to.

When he was done he put on his huge bathrobe and walked back out to the terrace. Once outside he donned a pair of shorts and lay down. The sun would dry him quickly enough. He picked up the phone and dialed his nephew.

"Hello, uncle. What do you want now?"

Fat Jimmy didn't like his tone of voice, but he wasn't interested in getting into it with the boy at the moment. "I want to go uptown this afternoon, and I want you with me."

"Yes, uncle, I'll be there. What time?"

"Two o'clock. And bring me a napoleon. Get it in Little Italy at Bella Dora's."

Fat Jimmy always wanted to be in the mob, he just didn't have the balls to do what was required. When the other kids were rooting for Eliot Ness he was rooting for Al Capone. He'd known John Gotti, senior and junior. But he wasn't cut out for it. His size would've made it difficult to dodge the occasional bullet often associated with that lifestyle, so he settled for running his little empire from this tiny piece of the world at the very tip of Manhattan. His years of trading commodities had shown him where the real money is. The biggest crooks didn't squeeze people for a few bucks or break legs in a dark alley loan sharking. They did it in a suit in front of everybody. And they did it on Wall Street.

So here he was, a wealthy man with a bit of power all about to go down the toilet because of his imbecilic nephew.

He walked over to his desk, opened the top drawer, and took out his gold trading badge, which used to be worth something in the glory days of commodities trading. It took him ten years of hard work and bad feet to earn it. It allowed him to trade in all the pits from coffee, sugar, and cocoa, to cotton, oil, gas, gold, anything. In his heyday on the floor, traders would run out of a pit when they saw Jimmy bringing paper in. His enormous size would literally push half a dozen brokers out of the trading area during a busy session. People complained to the board, but what can you do? They couldn't fine him for being fat and they couldn't prevent him from trading.

But now most of the pits were closed anyway, having gone electronic, and the others were sure to follow soon. People would trade the world's wealth from their own offices. The concept of open free-enterprise had taken a strange twist in this new world of computers. He had sold most of his seats recently when the mergers and buyouts took place and the prices went through the roof. But that wasn't enough for him. The anger and frustration he had felt most of his life could not be quelled with something as simple as money. He needed to feel powerful and to be feared. On the floor he had felt both. Now he only felt lonely and impotent.

At a quarter to two the nephew arrived. He let himself in and went out to the patio and joined his uncle, who had fallen asleep on the lounge chair.

"Uncle Jimmy, wake up."

Jimmy stirred. "Huh? What time is it?"

"Almost two."

"What? Why didn't you wake me earlier? I've got to get dressed."

He waddled into the apartment and entered his bedroom just as the buzzer rang. "Pick up the house phone in the kitchen," he shouted, "and tell them we'll be right out."

Skinny Jimmy did so and then went out to the terrace to make himself a drink. He decided to switch to Tangueray and tonic, mixed himself a strong cocktail, and added a lime wedge. He took a sip. Refreshing.

A few minutes later Fat Jimmy came out onto the terrace. The transformation was remarkable. There stood a large, but extremely well-dressed man. The suit was cream-colored, with a pink handkerchief, the shirt light beige, the shoes and socks a matching dark brown, and the hat an off-white panama. He smelled of lilacs and gardenias and seemed to practically dance his way onto the patio.

"Let's go, we've got people to see."

His nephew downed the drink in two gulps and followed him out the door.

Chapter Nineteen

Marty couldn't hide the awe Lowell's limousine instilled. It had more amenities than his apartment and was almost as big. Andy dropped them off at Marty's apartment. Marty bounded up the flights of stairs, and Lowell took them more slowly. Despite all of his walking, stairs got to his upper leg muscles.

Lowell waited until they were settled in Marty's room. He wanted the musician to feel at ease and unthreatened.

Marty gestured for him to sit on the futon.

"I'm sorry about all this," said Lowell.

"Yeah, shit happens."

"They took your stash, huh?"

The musician laughed. "Oh don't worry about that. I learned years ago never to put all your eggs in one basket." He walked over to the wall next to his computer table and removed a small piece of the wood molding. Behind it was a space containing another small box, which he took out, replacing the piece of wood. "You won't tell your friend the lieutenant about this, will you?"

"Scout's honor." Lowell raised three fingers.

"Yeah, live long and prosper."

He opened the box and took out a small baggie and a pipe. After loading the substance in, he took a lighter from his pocket and inhaled what looked to the astrologer like a very large amount. He held it for a few seconds, and then blew it out. A moment later he coughed a few times. "Boy, I needed that! Want a hit?" He extended his arm and offering the pipe to Lowell.

Lowell laughed and shook his head. "No thanks."

"You ever smoke?" Marty took another puff.

"Sure, years ago. But I don't think it would fit my lifestyle now."

"Well, if you change your mind, feel free. You know, in the early days you could smoke this shit and it would take away your memory, at least temporarily. Everybody that worked for the government or the AMA said it would lead to senility and make you stupid. But, hell, even that was a lot of bullshit. Turns out marijuana actually prevents Alzheimer's."

He took another puff. "Hell, it even shrinks lung cancer in rats. They're studying it now to see if it can be used as a tumor blocker. But it's still illegal."

"Tell me about yourself," said Lowell.

"What's to tell?" He waved his arms around. "What you see is what there is. I'm a poor, aging musician with just enough faith or stupidity to continue to struggle."

"So why do you do it?"

"What am I going to do, work in a shoe store?"

"A lot of people do."

"Yes, and those are the ones who come to the clubs and concert halls after work and listen to people like me. This is what I do. I can't suddenly become someone else. Do you think I'm happy living like this? I'm middle-aged, I have no health insurance, no retirement fund, and at the moment, no job. Of course I want more from my life."

There was a mirror hanging over the kitchen sink. He walked over to it.

"I like him." He pointed at the mirror. "I really do. He's a nice guy, doesn't hurt children or dogs, and he shouldn't have to worry about money as much as he does. There are times I look at him and apologize for not being able to give him a better life. I know that probably sounds pretty strange to you, disassociating me from myself, but it's true. If I could, I would take a job that would allow him, the artist, to work and create without worry. But I can't split myself in two, as much as I wish I could. So I struggle with the basics in life and continue to write songs and sing. I don't think it's got anything to do with success or failure anymore. I'm way past all of that. It's just stubbornness and the inability to accept that forty years of struggle was all for nothing."

He got up and walked over to the window and looked out on the deserted street. "They're planning to truck Manhattan's garbage across 72nd Street and up York Avenue twenty-four hours a day and ship it on out of the city on barges right up the street from here. Did you know that?"

"Yes, I am aware of the mayor's long-term plans for the city."

"Do you approve?" Marty's was ready for a fight.

"No, I do not approve. I think that in his zeal to modernize New York and leave behind a legacy to satisfy his humongous ego, the mayor has handed the city over to the landlords and banks, and destroyed the very flavor and diversity of Manhattan. And I believe that returning the garbage to this part of the city will quite simply destroy this neighborhood and much of the Upper East Side."

"Hmm…" The wind sucked out of his fury…"I figured you for one of them. Guess I was wrong."

"Why, because I have money?"

Marty nodded.

"Being rich isn't a crime in America."

"No, being poor is."

The air conditioner began to grumble. Marty walked over to it and hit it on the side. The noise got louder for a moment and then ceased.

"If your life was so hard, why didn't you change direction?"

"You can't give yourself a time limit in the arts. You have to do what you think is right until one day it's wrong."

"What do you mean?" asked Lowell.

"When I first came to New York in the seventies the first place I headed for was the Village. I had read everything there was to read about Phil Ochs, Eric Anderson, and especially Dylan. Even though I was a classical and jazz trained pianist my heart was in folk-rock. I went to Folk City every Monday night for years to play my original songs on their open-mic night. I was so good I was allowed to play three songs. Most of the acts only got to do two. Then I would walk the several miles home, often in the rain or snow, to save the bus fare. It would often take two hours or more. But I didn't care. I thought it would fuel my art."

"Did it?"

"Who knows? I had a lot of colds during those years. Eventually I did headline there, and I played the Bitter End, Kenny's Castaway's, and all the Village hotspots. Then I moved *uptown* to where they said the money was. Only I never could find it. I learned to eke out a living as a piano player and kept waiting for someone to notice me. I was always behind in my bills. I got evicted half a dozen times, and tossed out of every bank in Manhattan. One day I looked in the mirror and saw an aging hippie looking back. That's when I realized I was out of time."

"What about that thing with Freddie, what really happened?"

"Freddie was a jerk. He was always a jerk. Did you know that I knew him in high school, long before he became Rocket Fire? He was a prick then, too. He would take any woman he wanted, even if she was his best friend's girl. He didn't care. They liked Freddie, and he took advantage of any woman who didn't scream *rape* loud enough. He was a pig."

"So why did you work with him?"

"I don't think many people realize how hard it is to be in the arts. In order to make a living, a musician must work all the time, unless you become famous. When you're offered a gig like playing keys for Rocket Fire, with a steady income and guaranteed months on the road, you jump at it."

"Freddie must have wanted to help you out."

"Freddie never wanted to help anyone but Freddie. It was the drummer, Johnny Kanter, who recommended me for the gig. He and I were friends. We used to jam together late at night at the clubs and dug each other's sound. Freddie didn't want to bring me in at all. They had a big fight about it, but they couldn't get anyone else in time, so Freddie agreed. Then in Buffalo he hooked up with Mike Tanner, the keyboardist from the Mollies.

The band had just broken up and he was looking for a job, so Freddie threw me off stage and hired Mike. Nice business."

"Did you ever try to do anything else?"

"Sure. I was a bicycle messenger, cookie salesman, bartender, a singing waiter, secretary, dishwasher, delivery boy, clothing salesman, a cab driver, a fruit packer, a short order cook, and a truck driver."

"Wow," said Lowell, "that's a lot of jobs."

"Yeah. And the next year…" He laughed.

"If you did win the money, what would you do with it?"

"If you had asked me ten or even five years ago there would be no doubt, I would put it all into my musical."

"You wrote a musical?"

The musician nodded. "Had to. There's no place in rock and roll for me now."

"And now what would you do with the money?"

"Well, hell, now it's worth so much money I could buy a home and put on the play. I haven't got that much time left, so it's now or never."

"Is your show any good?"

"Why don't you decide?" He handed Lowell a few typed pages and his MP3 player, after first cleaning the earpieces with alcohol.

"This is a copy of part of the score and a synopsis. Why don't you listen to it while I run down to the store for a minute? If you like the music and the story you can read the script too."

Lowell positioned the earpieces in place. "You don't mind leaving me here?"

"Why? I got nothing worth stealing. And besides," he smiled, "I doubt that this is the first time you've been here alone."

He went out the door, closing it behind him.

Lowell picked up the synopsis, started the CD, sat back on the futon, and listened.

Chapter Twenty

The band members of Rocket Fire were all married and attempting to live a semblance of a normal life, at least off the road. Some lived their lives around the New York area, others in New England, but they had held onto joint ownership of a large rambling colonial in a small town in the Hudson Valley. That was where they lived while rehearsing or recording their records. The basement was a fully equipped multi-track, state-of-the-art recording studio. They had done some of their best work there over the years.

Andy pulled the limo into the circular driveway and around to the front of the building. Lowell got out and walked to the front door. He was about to ring the bell when the door opened and a barefoot young woman, clad in tiny green shorts and a white tank top, bounded past him and ran across the ragged, gravel driveway as if it were made of cotton. He watched her run.

"Who are you?"

The voice startled him. He turned back toward the door. "David Lowell. I'm investigating Freddie Finger's death."

"Oh yeah, Latner told us you'd be by. I'm Richard Polk, guitarist. Come on in."

He stood aside as Lowell entered the house. The man's face clearly revealed that he was past middle-age but with his obviously dyed, shoulder length black hair, and his t-shirt, jeans, and sneakers, he gave an appearance of being much younger.

"The guys are downstairs in the studio. Come on, I'll take you there."

They walked to the back of the house and down a flight of stairs. As they descended, Lowell could barely make out the muted sound of a rock song emanating from the basement. At the bottom of the stairs was a thick double door with a red light lit up on top.

"We've got to wait a minute, they're recording a track."

A few moments later the red light went off. Polk opened the door and they entered. The recording room had a couch and several arm chairs scattered about. The detritus of rock and roll everywhere: wires, stands, guitars, microphones, and amps strewn about. A baby grand Steinway piano looked out of place in this technological mayhem. A pinball machine and an air-hockey game stood along a far wall.

"Hey, guys, this is that detective Latner told us would be around."

The drummer played a drum-roll, and then hit a cymbal. "Oh, a detective. Well, this is getting more exciting every day. Johnny Kanter." He saluted with a drum stick. "You already met Ritchie." He pointed to the couch where two other long-haired older men sat. "That's George Fredrick, bass, and William Eagleton, keyboards."

Most of these men were several years older than Lowell, yet he felt like an old man in the company of teenagers. What a strange creature is rock 'n roll. Forever young.

"Can I ask you guys some questions about Freddie?"

"Sure." Kanter got up from his stool and sat in an armchair. "But only if we're suspects." He winked.

"At the moment everyone in Freddie's life is a suspect."

Kanter laughed. "This might be the hardest case you ever worked on."

"Why is that?"

The four band members looked at each other, as if silently trying to decide what information they would, and would not give. Lowell waited patiently. Finally, a brief nod from each.

Kanter spoke. "Well, the truth is, a lot of people didn't like Freddie. He was…difficult in a lot of ways."

Ritchie lit a cigarette and blew the smoke into the middle of the room. "Yeah, difficult." He laughed. "But talented as hell."

"How did you all get along with him?"

Again the silent looks.

Ritchie blew another cloud out, then snuffed out the cigarette in the tin ashtray on the table. "We're a band, Mr. Lowell. And a band is like a family. We have our problems, but we don't turn on each other."

"I understand. I'm only trying to get to the bottom of this. Can any of you think of a reason someone would want Freddie dead?"

Ritchie lit another cigarette. "I'm sure by now you know that Freddie wasn't the nicest person on the planet. He stepped on a lot of toes in his life, and I imagine someone wanted to return the favor."

Lowell tugged on his ponytail. "Only it wasn't his toes that got shot."

"Look, at one time or another we've all had our disagreement with Freddie. But we've lived and worked together for a long time. Freddie was like a brother to us all."

"What's going to happen to you now?"

Kanter got up and started to pace. "We're not sure. We have another album about to come out. We're going to have to do something."

"Won't you all make a lot of money from it?"

The drummer shrugged. "We'll do okay, but only Freddie and Ritchie, who wrote the songs, will make any real money from ASCAP, and they get the lion's share of the record sales. The rest of us rely on touring to make it."

"And without Freddie, there's no tour?"

This time most of the musicians looked at the floor, not each other.

Ritchie spoke. "Well, we may try to find a substitute, not that anyone can ever really replace Freddie."

Lowell tugged on his ponytail. "You mean another front man to do Freddie's act? Is that possible?"

Several of them nodded.

Ritchie blew a smoke ring. "A lot of bands continue after the original members die or leave. The band's name is like a trademark that can continue to earn for years."

"I read that you guys had thought about replacing Freddie even before he died. Any truth to those rumors?"

Their silence said it all.

"I'll take that as a yes."

Kanter started to pace again. "Mr. Lowell, don't think badly of us. This is a business like any other, it's how we support our families and put our kids through college. Freddie was moving on to other things. He wasn't that interested in the band anymore. He had more money than he could spend in three lifetimes, and he was concentrating on TV gigs, and more outside activities. The rest of us need to work or we'll go broke. And if Freddie didn't want to tour, there was no tour."

"Unless you replaced him."

"So now we're all suspects?" asked Ritchie.

Kanter returned to his drum kit. "Hey, great. I always wanted to be the bad guy in the movies." He hit the cymbal.

Lowell eyed the bandmates.

Ritchie blew out a cloud of smoke. "What else do you want from us?"

"Could I have your birth information? Date, place, and time."

Kanter chuckled. "Oh, that's right, I forgot. Latner mentioned that you're an astrologer. I have no problem with that." He scribbled the information on a piece of music paper, and then handed it to the others. Only George, the bass player, didn't know his time of birth, but promised to check into it.

Ritchie walked Lowell to the front door. The girl with the green shorts was lying on her back on the lawn catching some rays, topless. As the limo pulled out she sat up and waved at Lowell. He waved back.

Chapter Twenty-one

Lowell took a Coke from the refrigerator in the limo and dialed his office.

"Starlight Detective Agency," said Sarah.

"Is Mort there?"

"And good afternoon to you, too. He's right here, hold on."

"What's up boss?"

"I want you to double check the birth information for the four surviving members of Rocket Fire. I'm emailing it now."

"Okay, where will you be?"

"I'm going for a drive, so just email it back to me, there's no hurry."

"I understand." He knew that when Lowell went for a drive he was seeking solitude and wouldn't answer his phone.

Lowell wanted this time in the car to think. He turned on the scenery to the drive up the California coast he had shared with Vivian, endless beach on one side, grass-covered hillsides on the other, but found it made him miss her, and turned it off.

If they had more time Lowell would have asked Andy to take the Taconic instead of the thruway. He loved the twists and turns of the parkway and the bucolic setting so close to the city. Rock outcroppings and reservoirs lined the road, and he made a mental note to ask the system's designer, Delaney, to produce screen images for him of that route. The limo was one of the few places he really could relax and enjoy the privileges of his wealth, something he unknowingly shared with the late Freddie Finger. Still Lowell was eager to get back to the office.

The car was completely sound-proof, bullet-proof, and could probably survive a small rocket attack, or so the designer had hinted. It was an office on wheels, equipped with all the tools of his main office, a concept he very much had in mind when buying it.

He looked at the astrolabe on his computer screen, constantly rotating the planets, to get his bearings. The Moon had just entered his 12th house, ruler of the unconscious, often a time of introspection. That was probably why he felt like running away for a while. Well, it was time to use his intuition, not his intellect.

He sat back and tried to relax. Mercury was still retrograde and he knew that delays were inevitable. But Freddie's death was big news, and everybody wanted results.

Mort sent the requested information about thirty minutes later. There was a question mark next to the birth time of one of the names. Lowell threw the information into his "in" pile. He'd get to it later.

He went back to the computer and punched in a horary chart, an ancient means of divination used by astrologers for centuries. He thought out his question quite carefully: *What was the true motivation behind the three killings?* Then he went to Solar Fire and hit "here and now," and printed the chart. But the horoscope didn't tell him much. *The aspects are contradictory and unclear. Saturn is exactly square the ruler of the 7th house, which implies that the reader,* Lowell, *is not seeing something clearly, and cannot answer the question until further information is at hand.* They drove for a while as he thought. Perhaps it was the way he had stated the question.

Maybe all three murders weren't related. Was Roland right? He reworded the question. *What was the true motivation behind Freddie's murder?* Enough time had passed so that the house cusps had moved perhaps sufficiently to reveal a different answer than before. He printed it.

He sipped the cold soda and stared at the paper. *This is much more direct and clear,* he thought. *Uranus, the ruler of the 2nd house, is exactly square Pluto, which is conjunct the ascendant. It was financial, there's little doubt about it. And Jupiter's prominence on the nodes shows that it involved a great deal of money. That rules out almost nobody. Everyone involved in this case, including Marty Winebeck, stands to make or lose a great deal of wealth with Freddie's death. Uranus in exact square to Pluto also indicates that there was something vengeful about Freddie's murder as well. But that too doesn't much limit the suspects either.* He gazed at the chart with an unfocused eye and just allowed the numbers and symbols to wash over his mind.

He had once given a lecture on the astute awareness of our unconscious. In it he had proposed that we always know what's best for us, if we could turn off the loud conscious voice and hear the whispers underneath. This is why he meditated twice a day. If he could relax and let the information in through the unconscious he could sometimes find the illusive answer to his questions.

Lowell realized they were close to the city, as Andy had to slow and brake occasionally. He put the charts away, turned off the computer screen, and finished his Coke as the limo approached Manhattan.

They got back to the office about six. Andy took the car and left.

Lowell entered the deserted office - Sarah and Mort had both gone home for the day - and settled into his room. He opened the drapes to allow the sunset full access to his world. Lately he enjoyed the little things in life more and more. Was it an aging thing? Or was he finally reaching some sort of peace within himself. He turned on the TV and was about to call Louie's to order dinner when he changed his mind and dialed the Carlyle.

◇ ◇ ◇

He picked her up at seven.

"Do you mind if we stop at my townhouse for a moment?"

She was dressed all in white. "Not at all, if you'll give me a tour."

"Andy, stop at home."

The townhouse was on 93rd Street between Lexington and Third, a brown and white house in the middle of a row of townhouses. There was a metal gate about twelve feet in front of the house, which allowed for a small front yard. He buzzed the intercom.

"Hello?" said a female voice.

"Julia, it's Mr. Lowell."

"Mr. Lowell? Just a minute."

The gate buzzed. He and Vivian entered the front yard.

"This is so cute," she said. "Why don't you put a table and a few chairs out here?"

"Because this is New York City. You don't sit out on the sidewalk anymore. Not since about 1948."

"Oh, nonsense, I would do it and I think it would be fun."

"Not once the neighbors knew you were sitting out here. They'd crush you with their love. I'll show you something that may make up for your disappointment."

He opened the front door to the house.

"Mr. Lowell, is that you?" A short dark-haired woman came to the top of the stairs and looked down. A TV could be heard in the background.

"Yes, Julia, I'm here with a guest but I'm only staying for a minute. You just go back to whatever it was you were doing."

"Okay." She disappeared.

They were standing in a foyer with twelve-foot ceilings and a giant chandelier.

"Come in." He took her by the arm. "This obviously is the front hall. The house was built in 1929 right before the crash. Its foundation is brick and limestone and the entire structure has recently been refortified."

She was looking at the staircase, circular and winding up to a second, third, and fourth story.

"There is even a small elevator." He opened a small door and showed her the tiny lift. "Off to the left here is the living room."

They entered a large room that housed a Steinway grand, two opulent velvet couches, several chairs, a full wall of books, and a fireplace. He led her through a small den, bathroom, and the rest of the first floor until they reached the kitchen in the back of the house.

It wasn't too large, but had a center island and loads of counter space. Not an inch was wasted. There was a back door with a curtain across the window that reminded her of the 1950s.

"Here," he said, opening the door and turning a light switch, "maybe this would be a better place to sit than the front of the building."

It was a garden, small by California standards, but huge for Manhattan, framed on all three sides by tall wooden slab fences. There was a table with a built in umbrella, half a dozen chairs, a state of the art barbeque, and a shed. The lawn was perfectly kept, edged with colorful shrubs and many different kinds of flowers.

"The garden is one of Julia's pet project," he said. "She loves having this little bit of earth to play with."

"Oh, David," Vivian took his hand, "this is wonderful. But why would you stay in that office when you live here?"

"Austerity is often as much the parent of genius as inspiration. I get distracted here and start daydreaming. In the office there is only work. I must differentiate between the two or I could get lost."

He showed her the upstairs, four bedrooms, another den, and a workout room. The four bathrooms were spectacular, with a Jacuzzi in each.

The basement held his three room at-home office.

◇◇◇

They ate at a quiet neighborhood Italian restaurant. The ambience was subdued and the food terrific. They arrived early enough to be seated at once. There were only twelve tables in the place, and by the time they finished each was occupied, and there were about a dozen couples waiting. They took no reservations, accepted cash only and had a huge delivery business.

Over dinner they kept the conversation light, chatting about easy things, like where they went to college, favorite movies, and foods. After they had eaten Vivian could no longer contain herself.

"What do you think is going on?"

The detective was slowly stirring a packet of sugar into his espresso. He looked at her. With her brave exterior it was easy to forget that she had just lost her father. Her veneer was holding, but just barely.

"I wasn't close to my father," she said, "not as a child, anyway. My mother kept us apart and forbid me to see him for many years. It wasn't until recently that we began to spend time together. I finally forgave him for leaving us and learned to love him. It's such a fucking, god-damned shame." She started to cry softly. "It took us so long to get together and now he's gone."

She leaned against his shoulder, her head buried in his sport jacket, muffling her sobs. He gently patted her head. She looked up at him, her make-up smeared and running down her cheeks.

"You're going to owe me for a cleaning." He pointed to a round reddish-brown stain her mascara had left on his jacket.

She laughed, and then cried: "I'm sorry," she sobbed. "I'll pay for it."

"I'm only kidding, silly."

"I know." She wiped her eyes with a handkerchief. "But I thought I'd play along." She blew her nose and tried to control her sobs. "You remind me of him. Maybe it's your age. There's something about your generation that's different than mine. You're more compassionate, gentler."

"It was the times. The world was different in the sixties and seventies than it ever was or probably ever will be again."

"Why is that?" Her crying subsiding, now that her Gemini attention was on something interesting.

"Well," he sat back, taking on a professorial demeanor, "first of all we were the only winners of the Second World War. Europe was destroyed. Even the other victors were devastated financially and morally. China was bombed out and in the middle of a civil

war, with the rest of Asia in a state of chaos and horror following ten years of Japanese rule. Russia was bankrupt, India was
fighting for its independence, and everyone was looking toward
the U.S. to bail them out. Even our new enemies behind the
Iron and Bamboo Curtains were secretly cutting deals for food
and supplies. From 1945 on, this country relished in its role as
military and cultural ruler. Everyone wanted blue jeans and a
Coke."

"Okay," she sipped her cappuccino, "so we were the fat cats,
I get it."

"And the baby-boomer generation grew up in a society of
previously unknown wealth and growth. Because of FDR's
programs a generation earlier, America had social security,
unemployment benefits, and a sense of sanctuary and serenity.
There was a sugar coating to everything from advertisements
to government reports. We became the America Hollywood
had invented. Levittown with its picket fences and suburban
splendor was everyone's dream. We could finally shrug off the
Great Depression and the Second World War and live in Never
Never Land".

"So what happened?"

"The Bomb. Underneath all the prosperity and the security
was a collective nervous breakdown waiting to happen."

"And did it?"

"Did you hear tales of the sixties, of all sides of it?"

"When I was growing up in California you didn't hear about
much else."

"I'm convinced that the sixties was a collective nervous breakdown. I'm discussing that period of history and how astrology
played a role at a lecture next week. That era wasn't just about
sex and drugs. It was one of the most politically volatile eras in
man's history."

"Do you think my father's death could have been politically
motivated?"

"I don't know, but I haven't ruled out any possibilities. But
I promise you that I won't quit until I find out who did this."

After dinner they walked a few blocks until Vivian got tired. Andy, ever-present, pulled over when Lowell signaled. When they got to the hotel he was about to voice some platitude about her always being good company, when she put her lips on his. They kissed for a few moments, and then she pulled back.

"David, would you like to come up to my room?"

He could hardly catch his breath as he nodded.

Once they were in her suite there was no talking. She approached him directly and with great passion. They kissed, playing tag with their tongues. They went into the bedroom, dimly lit with only the distant light from the bathroom. She eased him out of his shirt and caressed his chest. He unconsciously tightened his stomach muscles.

She slowly took off her clothes, until she stood naked, her body outlined by the pale lamination. He removed the rest of his clothing, took her by the hand, and they lay on the bed.

He was painfully conscious of their age difference. His body, over fifty, could not hide its true identity. He discovered how difficult it is to hold in a paunch while lying down. They touched, and kissed, and explored.

When she was ready, they made love. She was ferocious, almost violent. Her body arched and relaxed, over and over. There was some primal need he was fulfilling, though he wouldn't think about it like that for days.

It had been so long. Not since his divorce almost eight years before. Feelings swelled in him, dangerous feelings. Twice they made love. And twice tears filled his eyes.

Finally spent, they fell asleep in each other's arms and awoke six hours later the same way.

Chapter Twenty-two

The next day Lowell was already at work when Sarah entered with Mort trailing behind.

Sarah opened the door and stuck her head out. "Breakfast is here."

"Bring it in here. And Sarah, the next time you get flowers for your desk bring a bunch in for mine as well."

"Boss?"

"Just want to spruce up the place a little."

Mort and Sarah exchanged a quick glance.

They ate together, Lowell filling Mort in on the case so far. He told him about the wives, the band members, the managers, the Bowie bonds, and the rather bizarre wager between Marty Winebeck and the nine other musicians.

"This isn't going to be our easiest case." Lowell tugged on his ponytail. "I need accurate information about all of these people, and you must find me Tracy's birth year."

"How is it, running around with Pete Sampson, Barron Dickens, and Bobby James?" Mort was obviously star struck.

"They're interesting people."

"And how about Vivian Younger? You haven't mentioned her at all."

"Oh, she's a very nice woman." He looked down at his pancakes.

Sarah and Mort exchanged another look.

Breakfast was over and Lowell and Mort got to work. There was much to coordinate between them, so Mort was stationed at the second computer in Lowell's office. The number of suspects was ridiculous. Freddie had pissed off so many people it was going to take a lot of time to sift through it all. And Lowell needed the birth information of all of the players.

At noon Sarah brought in a bouquet of mixed flowers in a vase and placed it on the edge of Lowell's desk.

About an hour later Sarah buzzed. "Mr. James is here to see you."

"Send him in."

"Bobby James?" asked Mort.

Lowell nodded.

The door opened and Bobby entered.

"Linguini with white clam sauce," said the psychic.

Bobby turned and looked at him. "I was just thinking about having that for lunch, although it was with a red sauce."

Mort looked at Lowell and shrugged. "Monochromatic." He pointed to his eyes.

"Huh?" said Bobby

"Color blind," replied Lowell.

"Bobby James, my god." Mort extended his hand. "I'm a big fan."

"Bobby, this is my friend and assistant, Mort."

Bobby shook Mort's hand.

"So what brings you to our neighborhood?" asked Lowell.

"I was on my way downtown so I figured I'd stop off and see if you had gotten anywhere. I've only got a minute, but as you can imagine, it's kind of important to me, to all of us. I told the others I'd report back."

Lowell filled him in with what he knew so far, which wasn't really much, while Mort sat agog like the over-aged fan he was.

"So you finally found Marty Winebeck, huh?"

"Actually, it was Mort who found him for me. This is the best computer guy I've ever known."

"Is that right?"

"Well, you know," said Mort, sheepishly, "it wasn't really that hard."

"Marty Winebeck. What's he up to?"

Lowell didn't quite know how to answer that. "Well, he's still in the music business, sort of."

"What's he do?"

"He performs and writes."

"Huh, he ever get anywhere?"

"Not by your standards, no."

"He never did make it?"

"Freddie pretty much put him out of business for a long time." He didn't mention the bizarre wager Marty and his friends had made.

"Well, rock 'n roll's a damn hard place. Do you think he had anything to do with the murders?"

"I don't know yet."

Bobby rose. "I've got to go. Keep me in the loop, okay?" He extended his hand to Mort. "It was nice meeting you."

"Likewise."

"Say, how about the wives? Could they have done it?"

"Well," said Lowell, "they're both still in the active file, but the second Mrs. Finger has sued the third Mrs. Finger three times. The third Mrs. Finger in turn sued back once. I don't think they could get out of each other's way long enough to commit murder, except maybe of each other."

"Call if there's anything I can do."

He shook hands with Lowell.

"The many wives of Freddie Finger," said Bobby, as he headed toward the door. "It could be an HBO series."

Chapter Twenty-three

Lowell and Roland were sitting at a coffee shop on Second Avenue near the precinct.

"You've got to get me something," said Roland. "You talked me out of arresting Marty Winebeck, so now where do we go?"

"Marty didn't do it, at least not alone. There is no way his chart could be that off."

"You never make mistakes?"

"I do," admitted Lowell, "but astrology doesn't."

"Maybe this is one of those times you did. And what if he didn't do it alone? There were ten of them involved in this bet. One's dead. Got shot about ten years ago. The others are very much alive. And that's a lot of money for a few of them to split. I'm still going to keep an eye on him. At the very least he's now got a file as a K.P.S."

Lowell looked at him.

"A Known Pot Smoker."

"Isn't it a bit of overkill?"

"The law is the law."

"But smoking pot? Rockefeller isn't governor anymore, you know. You sure you're not just pissed off about Freddie?'

"In 1990 the number of arrests for marijuana use in New York City was five thousand. In 2010 that number had gone up to over fifty thousand, even though the number of smokers has remained virtually the same. It's not just me. Your liberal ideas just don't have much clout anymore."

"*Oh, Brave New World,*" said Lowell.
"*That has such people in it.*"
"Shakespeare, Lieutenant?"
"I'm a conservative, not an illiterate. What about the wives?"
"I'm checking on everybody."
"Did you know that Rose had a criminal record?"
"What for?"
"She was an actress."
"I knew that. But I didn't know it was against the law."
"And did you also know that while she was flying around the world doing her movies she was also doing a little smuggling on the side, mostly jewelry?"
"That I didn't know."
"She was either very lucky or very well connected, because she apparently did it for years and they never caught her."
"So how did you find out?"
"Right before she met Freddie she took a trip to Milan. She returned on the same plane as a suspected drug dealer the feds planned on busting at JFK. As luck would have it, her bag was identical to his and they pulled it along with the dealer's. When they opened it they found several pieces of expensive jewelry she could not account for and booked her."
"What happened?"
"They were more interested in getting the dealer and his supplier, and concerned that her involvement might confuse the case, so they quickly cut her loose with probation and no jail time. There was some talk about her and the assistant DA having a fling, but it never came to light. Six months later she was married to Freddie and didn't need to work anymore. I guess it's better to be pretty than smart."
"Well, she may have been a bad girl, but that doesn't make her a murderer."
"Somebody did it!" The cop was obviously annoyed.
Lowell took a bite of his jelly donut. "Time will tell."
"Time is the one thing I don't have."

"I already told you when I thought this would be solved. It will take until Mercury goes direct and I don't believe there's a thing we can do except muddle through."

"Ahh!" said a frustrated Roland, as he got up and walked out, leaving Lowell with the check.

Chapter Twenty-four

"Mercury retrogrades three times a year for about three weeks each time," said Lowell.

"A lot of my friends are into this stuff and they've all mentioned it. And it's all over the Internet. Explain that to me." Sarah flipped her red hair. "What does retrograde mean?"

"This is an oversimplification but imagine you're on a train moving forward and you pass another forward moving train. If you look out the window as you go by it appears that the other train is moving backwards. It's an optical illusion. When our orbit passes that of another planet, when that planet is on the opposite side of the Sun, it appears as if that planet is going backwards against the constellations. We call that retrograde motion. All the planets retrograde, except the Sun and the Moon."

"What does that mean for people?"

"Depending upon which planet it is, the energy of that celestial body is internalized and often difficult to express outwardly. When Mercury is in retrograde we experience a greater than usual number of electronic failures, difficulties with communications and transportation. You should leave extra time for travel, and expect delays. Subways, cars, planes are all susceptible to difficulties. You should not purchase any product involved in those areas, including cell phones, computers, cars, or clock-radios. One year during the same three week retrograde period, the main computer in the New York City post office department crashed, the mainframe for over thirty six thousand metro card machines went down and they had to each be reset by hand, the e-z-pass in New Jersey stopped working, and the Swiss, known world over for their precise timepieces, set all of their official state clocks ahead two hours instead of one at the start of daylight savings time. Mistakes abound and you should not sign important documents. Secrets are also often revealed while the change in direction is occurring. If you remember, it played a significant role in solving the Winston case."

"It affects everyone?"

"It affects the world, and thus it will affect you in some ways, although I find that many Geminis seem to do just fine during these periods."

"Whatever." She shrugged and went back to her desk.

A few minutes later she tried to call her sister on her cell phone but couldn't get a signal. Even on the landline she couldn't get through. "Mercury?" she asked aloud.

Lowell hated when Mercury retrograded. It made his thoughts move slower and information very difficult to uncover. Although he did find that if he just let things fall where they might during these times, somehow or other it always worked out. Still, it was frustrating and it wasn't his nature to just sit back and wait. These retrograde periods favored free-form creativity and spiritual matters. He favored clear thoughts and hard work.

He opened the folder containing the facts of this case. Besides the police papers and computer work Mort had done, there were several dozen astrology charts, which he separated into two piles: possible and improbable. Of course nothing was *impossible*, so he had no third pile.

There were the two ex-wives.

Tracy: dumb but conniving and probably capable of evil. But could she mastermind three murders? He doubted it. She didn't seem capable of thinking more than a step or two down the line. But he had often met people who were able to put on a front for years, fooling even their most intimate acquaintances. The natal chart would show the true personality, but Tracy had successfully confused the year of her birth, and without an accurate chart he was lacking the tools necessary to eliminate all doubt, so she stayed in the *possible* file.

Rose: the quiet type, passion bubbling under the surface. She was smart enough to do it, but what was her motivation? There was little she would gain, except for some more money, which didn't seem to interest her particularly. And if she was lying about suing the estate, how would she explain her change of heart now without bringing suspicion upon her? And what about Gene and Wally? How and why would she kill them?

And there was wife number one, Lilly, Vivian's mother. Mort had tracked down a verifiable birth date and Lowell had put her chart in the files. He would never mention this to Vivian, but he had to cover all bases. Lilly's astrology chart showed a sweet, good-natured soul. If anything she was more of a victim than either of the other two wives. He punched up the composite chart between Freddie and Lilly. It showed a Sun Venus conjunct in the 8th house of sexual partners. Theirs might actually have been a marriage of love, at least at the start. That's why they were able to produce someone as lovely as Vivian. Lilly didn't have it in her to do this.

There must have been hundreds of people who wanted Freddie dead. He couldn't pick through each, it would take forever.

He picked up his notebook and began reading through it. When he didn't know what else to do he went through everything systematically. Bobby wasn't wrong. Rock n' roll sure is a nasty business. About all he could do now was probe the various options opened to him.

He picked up the phone and punched in some numbers.

"Morgan Stanley," said a female voice.

"Roger Bowman."

"One moment, I'll try that extension."

"This is Roger.

"It's Lowell."

"Starman, how are you? How are the planets?"

"They're still up in the sky. Tell me what you know about the Bowie bonds."

"The Bowie bonds, huh? I guess you're working on the rock n' roll killings?"

"Good guess. Tell me what they're all about and how secure they are, who put it together, you know."

"How soon do you need it?"

"Yesterday."

"Alright, I'll call you back. It may take a day or so, we've been having problems with our computers."

"Somehow I'm not surprised. Let me know when you've got something."

He hung up and called Vivian. When he suggested dinner she balked.

"I'm tired of just eating out. Let's do something New Yorkish."

"New Yorkers go to restaurants."

"Not all the time."

"Yes, all the time."

"Well, I want to do something else tonight."

"Like what?"

"I don't know, go to a show or something."

"People from New Jersey do those things."

"Then let's pretend I'm from New Jersey."

Lowell made some calls and they went to a new musical. A friend of his was one of the producers and they sat in the third row. The seats were excellent. The show wasn't.

Afterwards they had a drink at Sardi's, just like tourists. It was a little uncomfortable, as it often is when a love affair begins. But neither let it interfere.

"I have a message for you from your father's wife."

She was drinking a martini with several large stuffed green olives. She pierced one with a toothpick and nibbled at it.

"Which one? Number two or number three?"

"Tracy."

"Oh, good old number two." She picked up her glass. "What did she have to say?"

"She told me to tell you that 'Mom' says hello."

She laughed so hard that she spilled about half the drink. "Mom? Did she actually say that? Oh that's a good one."

The bartender hurried over and cleaned up the mess.

"She's only a few years older than me. When she was married to my father I was in my teens and had to keep my boyfriends away from her or she would flash them. Mom, that's funny."

"You weren't close to your father's wives?"

"Rose is okay. I think she's about my age. I always thought of her as a younger sister. By the time she came into the picture I was already in my late twenties and not much of a threat for my father's affections. In fact, Rose and I were friends, sort of, for a while. But Tracy was really into a power struggle regarding my father."

"With you?"

"With everybody. She would create a scene if he flirted with another woman and at the same time I wouldn't give you a nickel for her fidelity."

"Would she have any reason to want your father dead?"

"My father? No, not that I can think of. But if Rose were to die suddenly you might not have to look too far."

"So I've heard."

Chapter Twenty-five

Tracy showed up unannounced a little after noon on Tuesday. She walked into the office with the air of aristocracy, a jacket thrown nonchalantly over her shoulder and a cigarette holder in her hand. *All that's missing,* thought Sarah, *is a white poodle.* She wore a flimsy white blouse opened two buttons below decency and a pair of green pants so tight that Sarah thought she must be numb from the waist down.

Sarah showed the ex Mrs. Finger into Lowell's office.

"How nice of you to drop in on me."

Sarah snickered audibly as she left.

"Do sit down."

She hung her jacket over the back of the chair and sat, dropping her purse on the floor. She took the cigarette holder out of her mouth and put it in her purse.

"I thought I would stop by and see how things were progressing. Have you had a chance to delve into the heart-broken widow yet?"

"I interviewed Rose, just as I did you."

"Oh, you don't know her. She puts on that sincere straight-laced image, but she's dangerous. And she's more than able to kill for profit."

She took out a pack of Marlboro's and a lighter, shook one from the pack and popped it into her mouth. "And," she lit the thing, "she wouldn't think twice about stringing him up." She blew out a huge cloud.

"I don't really allow smoking in here."

"And I appreciate you bending the rules for me." She blew out another puff.

"I didn't mean…"

"And another thing, I'll bet if you look into her financial records you'll find enough discrepancies for a motive right there. I'll bet she's been ripping him off for years."

She blew another giant cloud in his direction and looked around for an ashtray. There was a candy dish on the desk presently void of goodies. She pushed the cigarette into the dish only partially putting it out. Then she got up and walked over to his chair, sitting on the edge of the desk, very close to Lowell.

"Maybe together we could get her," she leaned over and whispered in his ear.

The intercom buzzed.

Lowell grabbed it. "Yes, what?"

"Max is on line one," said Sarah, "but I told him you were tied up and…"

"Thank you, I'll talk to him. I'm sorry, I've got to take this call," he told Tracy.

She sat back in her chair.

"Uh, I really need some privacy here."

She didn't stir.

He picked up the phone. "Hello, Max, what can I do for you?"

"I've got a client's chart I'd like you to look at for me," said the acupuncturist.

"Okay, what are the birth information and the symptoms?"

Lowell took down the information and promised to call back with his diagnosis. Then he hung up. He looked over at his guest.

"Tracy, what do you want from me?"

"I want you to get her for killing my Freddie." She began to take another cigarette from her pack.

He shook his head and she pushed it back in.

He stood up and walked around the desk, took her by the arm and gently, but forcefully, walked her to the door.

"I tell you what, let me look into a few things and I promise I'll call you personally once I know something."

She was not happy with the results of her visit, but his grip was firm and his voice unbending, so she acquiesced. She was used to getting her way and not accustomed to having her sexuality ignored. She didn't like it.

Chapter Twenty-six

For the tenth day that month the temperature topped ninety degrees. Global warming was the smelly, sweaty, elephant in the room in almost every conversation in the city.

Lowell and Vivian left Lowell's office and would have taken a walk but for the oppressive environment. They were about to get into the limousine, ever present with Andy at the wheel waiting, when a blue Chevy pulled up and the back door opened. Skinny Jimmy came out, gun in hand.

"Get in the limo, both of ya." He aimed the gun directly at Vivian.

Lowell thought about disarming him, but he couldn't risk Vivian's safety, so he followed the man's orders.

The man sat at the desk chair in front of the computer. "You two sit over there." He pointed to the leather seat. When they were all seated in Lowell's car Jimmy said: "Tell your driver not to try any funny stuff or I'll waste the broad right here."

"Broad?" said Vivian.

"Where do you want to go?" asked Lowell.

"I'll let you know. Just tell him to head out the Long Island Expressway and I'll tell you the exit later."

Lowell picked up the phone. "Andy, we've got a situation back here."

"I know, I saw him follow you in. Want me to do anything?"

"No, just do what he says to the letter, understand?"

"Sure. Uh, Boss," Andy said softly, "are we on speaker?"

"No."

"We got a tail, a blue Chevy. And I think, maybe a second car as well."

"I understand. Just follow his instructions and head toward the L.I.E. Take the tunnel."

"No you don't," said Jimmy, "take the Triboro Bridge."

"Take the bridge," Lowell repeated into the phone.

"And no funny business." Jimmy waved the gun in Lowell's face.

"Would you mind putting that thing down?" asked Vivian. "We're not going to do anything."

"Just shut up and sit there."

"Want to tell me what this is all about?" asked Lowell.

"Just shut up. You'll find out soon enough."

They rode in silence for about fifteen minutes.

"I'm thirsty," said Vivian.

"You mind if I get her a bottle of water?"

"Yeah, just don't try anything," replied Jimmy. "I know all about you."

"What does he mean?" asked Vivian.

"I believe I've met this gentleman's associates recently in Soho, if I'm not mistaken."

Lowell opened the refrigerator, took out a bottle of water and handed it to Vivian.

"You want one?" he asked Jimmy.

"No, I don't want nothin' except that you keep your mouth shut."

Traffic was awful. They drove bumper to bumper at speeds ranging from ten miles an hour to seventy, yet always with the cars no more than a few feet behind each other.

After about an hour Jimmy said: "Tell him to get off at exit sixty-eight and then make a left."

"If we could just talk about this," said Lowell, "I'm sure we can come to some understanding."

"We'll come to an understanding, all right. You'll understand just fine in a little while."

Lowell picked up the phone and slowly repeated the instructions to Andy. His eye was on the astrolabe. The Moon was just about to go *void of course*, a time when the energy is disconnected and things often go awry. If he was going to get the chance this would be the time. He had noticed the gunman flex his fingers on the barrel of the gun a few times in recent moments. He would likely want to switch hands soon.

Jimmy obliged, and before his grasp on the barrel was tight, Lowell brought the phone down hard on both of the gunman's hands.

The gun dropped and landed on the floor near Vivian's feet. Jimmy leaned over to get it. Lowell put his left hand under Jimmy's shoulder, pushed up, grabbed his right forearm and twisted it down until Jimmy literally was lifted from his seat.

"Hey, cut it out, will ya?" he shouted.

Vivian leaned over and punched him in the jaw. His head hit the glass partition and out he went.

"Broad, huh? I'll show you who's a broad."

"That's a hell of a left," said Lowell.

"Girl's boxing champion, Catholic School's regional, three years running. Those nuns know how to fight."

Vivian picked up the gun and handed it to Lowell. "Now what?"

"We still have to find out what this is all about."

He removed the clip from the gun, checked the chamber, and put it in his pocket. Then he picked up the phone. "Andy, all under control back here. Can we lose the tail?"

"Sorry boss, there's no place to go. It's just one long straight line. And I've got a car on either side boxing me in."

"Okay, just keep rolling and don't stop no matter what."

"Gotcha boss. But we're not far from exit sixty-eight."

"I understand."

Lowell hung up the phone and thought for a minute.

"I've got an idea." He turned the dials at the control panel. "Just play along with me."

"Okay," replied the actress, ready to get into character. "Where are we?"

"Connecticut."

He turned the knob on the scenario machine until a New England moonlight oceanscape came into vision. He took the cell phone from Jimmy's jacket and put it in his own. Then he adjusted the watch on Jimmy's arm. He turned off the screen on his computer, tied his would-be kidnapper's hands together in front and, when he was satisfied that the stage was set, threw some water into Jimmy's face.

It took a few seconds for him to come around. "Where am I?"

"You're in my limousine. What's your name?"

"Jimmy."

"Jimmy what?"

"None of your business. Jesus, what did you hit me with?"

"I didn't hit you, she did."

"Hey," he put his bound hands on a bump on his head, "lighten up lady." He looked out the window. "Where the fuck are we?"

"Connecticut."

"What the fuck? Connecticut, are you crazy? How long was I out?"

He looked at his watch and cursed. Then he tried to look out the back of the car, but the rear window was darkened.

"Don't bother. We lost your companions hours ago. Nobody knows where you are. You're all alone now."

"Yeah, well fuck you. Wait till my uncle finds out what you did. Kidnapping's against the law."

"And what were you doing to us?" asked Vivian.

"Aw, I was just taking you out to the Island, that's all. I wasn't gonna hurt you. This is crossing state lines, fercrisake. That's a federal offense, ain't it?"

"Only if you're under eighteen," replied Lowell. "Who's your uncle?"

"None of your business." The fear showed quite clearly on his face. "But you'll find out soon enough."

"Listen, buddy," Vivian put on her act, "you're on your own now. Nobody is going to come to your rescue. You've got one chance to level with us or we'll put you somewhere they'll never find you."

"You're not gonna kill me," said Jimmy, assuredly.

"Really, and why not?" asked Vivian. "You were willing to kill us."

He turned to Lowell. "Keep her away from me, will ya? She's crazy."

"Is she right?"

"Aw, I wasn't going to hurt you. I just wanted you out of the way for a while, that's all."

"Yeah right," said Vivian. "No funny stuff or I'll waste the broad right here. Isn't that what you said?"

"You don't got to take everything so literal, do ya?"

"What do you want with us?" Lowell took the gun from his pocket and waved it in Jimmy's face.

"I ain't talking."

"Okay," Lowell turned to Vivian, "we'll be near that little town I mentioned. We can dump him there."

"Okay with me."

"Hey," said Jimmy, "you're a broad. You ain't supposed to think like that."

"Really? You kidnap us, you threaten us with a gun, and you probably murdered my father. Why wouldn't I want to bump you off, as you would say?"

"What? Murdered you father? I never killed nobody. I don't even know who your father is."

"My father is, was, Freddie Finger."

"Oh, him. I had nothing to do with that, I swear to you. I didn't kill him. I didn't kill nobody."

"So who did?" asked Lowell.

"I don't know." Jimmy was near tears. "I don't know nothin' about any murders."

"I don't know if I believe you." A thought came to Lowell. "Do you own a crimson sweatshirt with a hood?"

"No, why?"

"It's not important. And you had us attacked downtown."

"I was just tryin' to scare you. You didn't have to go all ape shit on us. Christ, you put Leo in the hospital. And one guy's shoulder ain't never gonna be the same."

The phone rang.

"Boss," said Andy, "we passed exit sixty-eight and the two cars are trying to box us in. What do you want me to do? There's a small rest area in three miles, and it looks like they're going to force us into it, unless you want me to speed up."

"Go ahead and stop there, we can dump the body. Just be ready to leave immediately."

"I understand."

Lowell took the gun and put it next to Jimmy's temple. "I want to know who killed Freddie."

"I don't know." Sweat starting to bead on his forehead.

"I'll count to three. One…"

"I swear I don't know."

"Two…"

"You got to believe me, I don't know!"

"Three." And he pulled the trigger.

"Ahhh!" shouted Jimmy, when he heard the clicking sound. But nothing happened. There was no bullet in the chamber. He sat back in the seat breathing heavily.

The blue Chevy had come along side the limo. There was a black Toyota directly behind. Andy didn't have much of a choice but to pull into the rest area. He weaved over to the right and took the ramp. The Chevy had pulled in front and the Toyota remained in back. Once they were off the highway the Chevy stopped, forcing Andy to do the same.

Two men exited the car, both holding guns. The rest area was deserted, except for a lone trucker apparently asleep in his cabin.

As soon as the car stopped Lowell opened the door. "Get out."

"What? Here? What the fuck am I going to do in Connecticut? You can't leave me here."

Lowell waved the gun in his face. "Get out!"

Jimmy did as he was told.

When he exited the car and saw his surrounding he was too confused to act for several moments. The two gunmen seeing Jimmy holstered their weapons and were walking over to where he was.

Lowell pulled the door shut, and Andy slammed on the gas, ramming the Chevy in front with the limo's reinforced steel bumpers and pushing it into a pole and out of his way. He drove the limo around it and was back on the highway before anyone could react.

The Toyota gave chase, but ate dust. Jimmy and the two gunmen jumped into the Chevy, but the car was useless.

Jimmy grabbed a cell phone from one of the two men and punched in a number.

Chapter Twenty-seven

Lowell called Lieutenant Roland and told him about their encounter. He and Vivian went to the precinct and looked through some mug shots, but they couldn't find their assailant. All they knew about him was that his name was Jimmy, and he had an uncle. He dropped Vivian at her hotel and went back to the office.

◇◇◇

Lowell was at his desk when the intercom buzzed. "Yes, Sarah?"

"Melinda's here."

"Send her in."

The door opened and a tall woman with long chestnut hair, dressed in a blue pinstriped skirt suit entered. At five foot eleven she towered over Lowell. She walked over to his desk and kissed him on the cheek. "Hi, dad. Just wanted you to know I'm in town."

"I'm glad you're back. How was Texas?"

"Hot, but not as bad as here! How is your case going?"

He told her about the attempted kidnapping.

"Are you alright? Why would someone try to kidnap you?"

"I don't know. I must be getting close to something." Lowell tugged on his ponytail and shrugged. "This is a difficult case. Not too many people liked Freddie Finger, and I've got more suspects than I know what to do with. And there is a large sum of money involved, but it's unclear who stands to benefit the most."

"Nobody stands out?"

He shook his head. "Not really. Although the comparative charts show plenty of animosity between Freddie and many of his people, there isn't a chart that points directly toward any one of them." He pushed a button on the intercom. "Let me get Mort in here." He looked at his daughter. "You look tired. I think that law firm is running you ragged."

"I'm okay, just a little jetlag."

There was a brief knock, and then Mort entered. "Melinda, what a pleasant surprise. How was your trip?"

"It was okay. A bit tiring, but that's what you get when you're low man on the totem pole." Melinda sat in a client's chair. "Dad, can you fill me in quickly?"

Lowell told her about the case and his plethora of suspects. "I think it's time to work the composite charts. I'm not getting anywhere with the individuals. Do you remember what I taught you about composites?" Melinda was his prize astrology student.

His daughter nodded. "Oh yes. You were quite adamant about their uses"

Mort tilted his head. "Composite charts?"

Lowell sat back in his chair. "The chart of a relationship between two people can be quite different from either individual's energy. There are several different horoscopes I look at including the composite chart, which is made up of the midpoints between all the planets in two people's natal charts. It shows the nature of the relationship and how the two will react together."

Mort thought about it. "Interesting, but how will that help you with this case?"

"Have you ever had a friend who starts to date someone, and their personality changes? You may still enjoy that friend's company alone, but not when they are together. A separate entity now exists, we call the relationship. You and Melinda may act one way when you are separate, but once you interact, that third creature now has a voice. And you may react to things differently than you normally would. If Freddie's death was the result of several people's actions, I may have to see it in the composite charts to truly understand the dynamics of how those people interact."

Lowell stood up and walked to the window. "Mort, what have you got for me?"

"Well, this may or may not be much, but I discovered something about the Mrs. Fingers numbers two and three that you may find useful. Did you know that while the two of them are outwardly fighting and suing each other, they have quietly put together an Internet business to sell Freddie's things?"

Lowell smiled widely. "How interesting. Maybe they aren't quite the enemies they pretend to be. Any luck finding the real birth information for the second Mrs. Finger?"

"I believe I have. According to the class records at Great Neck High School, Tracy Finger was born Evelyn Goodman. Luckily it was a local birth and easy to track down. She was brought into this world at North Shore Hospital on October 21, 1973."

"At least she had been honest about the day. Well done. How about the time?"

"I had to get into the old records at the hospital to get a glance at the birth certificate. They don't even add the older ones to computers. But I did manage to bluff my way in, and it said 9:32 a.m."

"Let's take a look." Lowell punched in the information for Tracy and then the combined chart of her and Rose. "See, Melinda, this is what I'm talking about. Neither of these two individual charts shows a vengeful nature, although Tracy has a Sun – Uranus conjunct, which could make her explosive and edgy. And Rose has the Moon in square to Uranus, so she also has a nervous and erratic side. It's probably what Freddie found appealing in both. But neither has a particularly bitter or callous nature.

"But in the composite chart it's another story. The Sun conjuncts Pluto, which can be a very powerful and even ruthless aspect. Interestingly enough it's found in Freddie's natal chart as well. But then, we are looking at the chart of two wives who, until only a few moments ago, we believed hated each other. This is not the composite chart of best friends, that's for sure. The composite chart certainly shows that to be true. No matter what else they may be involved in, these two do not like each other. So we must find out if there is something behind the animosity."

Mort's head bobbed up and down. "Won't you also have to do the composites for Marty Winebeck and the other eight musicians?"

"I suppose." Lowell groaned. "But the thought of sifting through the combination of charts nine people present is a daunting task. It could be any number of combinations before I hit upon one that rings true. The dynamics of a couple or a group are that different than that of the individual."

Lowell smiled. "I often wondered what Bonnie's life would have been like if she hadn't met Clyde."

"So you'll have to sift through all of the combinations?"

"Unless I get lucky." He sighed and turned to the computer. "Might as well get to work. Mort, see what you can do about finding the birth information for the other suspects."

"I'm on it." He rushed out of the office.

Melinda walked to the window. "This seems like a particularly frustrating case for you."

"This is a very Neptunian situation all around."

"Why Neptune?"

"As you know, Neptune is the most confusing and misdirecting of all the planets. It rules alcohol, drugs, music, and anything that is an illusion. It is most prominent in the arts. There was nothing real in any of this. Sixty-year-old musicians that look and act like they're twenty. Ex-wives and widows with more hate than love. And friends who perhaps weren't friends at all. The glimmer of stardom surrounded by Neptune's fog."

He tugged on his ponytail. "Have you thought about what we discussed?"

"I have. But I'm not sure I'm ready to go out on my own."

"If you ever decide to, you know you have my full support."

"Thanks, dad." She leaned over and kissed him on the forehead and left.

The rest of the day was filled with electronic problems of all sorts. The computers ran slowly and they had to reboot the system twice.

At four he had Andy drive him back to the Village.

◇◇◇

Rose was wearing a beige pantsuit when she answered the door. "Mr. Lowell, how nice to see you again so soon. Please, come in."

He entered and sat on the couch. "I won't be long. There are just a few more questions."

"Of course. Would you like some coffee?"

"No, thank you."

"And these questions couldn't be answered on the phone?"

"I thought it prudent to discuss it in person. It has come to my attention that you and Tracy have put together a company to sell Freddie's belongings over the Internet."

She crossed her legs. "That's true. And I'll bet you're wondering why two women who hate each other would go into business together." He nodded. "Don't think for a moment that this new business venture changes how we feel about each other. We just have a common interest and decided to pool our resources briefly."

"I thought money wasn't an issue for you?"

"I wouldn't contest the will, but what's wrong with selling some of Freddie's crap and making a few bucks? If we tried to compete it would be a mess. This way we can unload a lot of stuff and make Freddie's fans happy as well. There's nothing nefarious about it. Just a temporary truce."

Chapter Twenty-eight

Sarah had her coat on and was about to leave for the day when the front door opened. It was the first time she had actually met Vivian and was quite taken by her charisma. It's one thing to see someone up on the screen, but to be in the presence of a real star, someone who deserved that title, well, that was something else.

"How do you do?" Vivian extended her hand.

Sarah put hers out automatically.

"You must be Sarah? I'm Vivian. Is David, I mean Mr. Lowell, available?"

Sarah had never been speechless in her life. If anything she tended to be just the opposite. But try as she might not a single word came to her mind.

"I…uh…I," she giggled uncontrollably. "Oh," finally catching herself, "please forgive me, Ms. Younger."

"Vivian, please."

"Vivian, oh my, sorry. Let me tell him you're here."

Vivian laughed good-naturedly. "It's so nice to finally meet you. David has said such nice things about you."

"He has?"

"Oh, yes. The way he tells it he couldn't run this office without you."

"He couldn't? Well, I do keep thing in order for him. You know, he's a really smart guy, but he can be so disorganized."

"Genius often is," replied Vivian. "If I told you about some of the biggest stars and directors in Hollywood you'd be in hysterics. Some of them literally couldn't shop in a supermarket. God help them if something actually went wrong anywhere but on a movie set."

She spied Sarah's new shoes. "Those are fantastic."

Sarah beamed. "Do you like them?"

"Like them? My god they're absolutely stunning. Where did you get them?"

"On Eighth Street and Mercer. I'll show you, if you'd like?"

"I'd love that. How about tomorrow?"

Sarah just nodded, afraid she would start giggling again.

"How about noon? We can have lunch."

Sarah nodded again. "Great," she managed to spit out. "Let me tell him you're here."

Lowell rose as Vivian entered. "This is a pleasant surprise."

"As the old saying goes, I was in the neighborhood. Are you busy?"

"Always."

"Too busy for a quick dinner with me?"

"Don't you want to take a sight-seeing tour bus around the city?"

She smiled. "I've had my fill of being a tourist. A nice quiet dinner would suit me just fine."

Lowell called Andy who was waiting when they came out of the building.

"Where shall we eat?" asked Vivian.

"Any place you choose. What are you in the mood for?"

"How about Indian? They usually have a large vegetarian selection."

"Fine. We'll go to East 6th Street, the Indian restaurant capital of New York. There are about a dozen to choose from."

"God, when I leave New York I'd like to take the restaurants with me. I'm going to miss the variety when I get back to LA."

"One does get spoiled. There are thousands of restaurants in this city of every conceivable style. Whatever you can think of that you'd like to try, there's some place that makes it. Eating out is the main recreational activity."

"I don't doubt it for a minute," replied the tourist.

Dinner was subdued. Vivian seemed a bit withdrawn, but was still good company.

"David, do you mind just dropping me at the hotel? I'm tired and wouldn't be much fun. We could get together tomorrow if you're free?"

"Of course."

Lowell wasn't used to dating and even he, the clear-thinking astrologer, could not see where this relationship was going.

Chapter Twenty-nine

Fat Jimmy was drinking peppermint tea and eating a Granny Smith apple. He'd read somewhere that certain kinds of apples helped control acid reflux and he was trying different varieties. So far none of them had done much.

"Now, what did I tell you? Didn't I say I was going to take care of this guy? Didn't I?"

His nephew nodded.

"So you blew it a second time. Now do you think we're in the clear?" He pushed the table away and slowly stood up. "Call up the guys and have them meet us at the warehouse in Brooklyn."

An hour later they were outside a seedy rundown warehouse where they met up with two other men. It was situated near the docks on a dead end street in an undesirable area of Brooklyn. But that would change as the reconstruction of this borough continued. And Jimmy was counting on being bought out for a nice fat profit when the time came. In the meantime he used the building for a variety of purposes.

"Jeez, I haven't been out here in a while. It's really a shithole, isn't it?"

He went to the front door carrying a large family size bucket of Kentucky Fried Chicken. He fiddled with the keys until the right one fell in his hand and he twisted it into the lock. The door swung open and he started to enter when he realized that the door was too narrow for him.

"Open the freight door."

"Uh, I don't have the key with me," replied his nephew.

Fat Jimmy just looked at him and shook his head. He turned back to the doorway in front of him. By twisting sideways and inching his way in he was able to squeeze by.

There was a large table with several chairs around it. They all sat.

He looked around the table at his "gang" and shook his head again. It was enough to see the giant, at six five, supposed to be the muscle, with his shoulder in a sling, a shiner under his left eye, and bruises on his face and arms.

"Now listen, you morons," he started on his first chicken leg, "I want that guy and I want him now. This is the last time I want to hear that he escaped or beat you all up. Is that clear?"

"Yes, Mr. Jimmy," said several of them.

"All right then, here's the plan. And you better not screw it up."

◇◇◇

Andy pulled the limo around to the side entrance of the restaurant. He got out to stretch his legs when a short man approached him.

"Got a light?" asked the man.

"Yeah, sure." Andy got a lighter from his pocket. Although he had quit smoking almost five years earlier, he still carried a Bic wherever he went. Some habits die hard. He cupped both hands around the flame so the man could get a good light.

A very large man came up behind him and held a gun to the side of his head. "Just be cool and nobody gets hurt." The shorter man tied Andy's hands behind his back as a green car pulled up. The gunman waved toward the car. "Get in." Andy got in the back and it pulled away.

The short man got in the limo driver's seat and the large man got in the back.

Lowell and Vivian exited the restaurant. "There's Andy." Lowell pointed to the limo.

They were about to get in when Skinny Jimmy came up behind them holding his pistol. "Get in."

"What, again?" asked Lowell. "Isn't this redundant?"

"What?"

"Aren't you getting tired of this?"

"Just get in and shut up."

Lowell opened the door and saw the big man. "Friend of yours?"

Lowell and Vivian entered and sat. The large man had his right arm in a sling and a gun in his left hand. Lowell recognized him from his encounter in Soho.

Jimmy kept his gun aimed at Lowell. "No funny business this time."

Lowell reached for the phone. "Let me give my driver instructions."

"That ain't your driver. Put the phone down and sit back."

Lowell was worried. He knew Andy wouldn't voluntarily give up the car. "Where's my driver?"

"Never mind. I'd worry more about myself if I were you. Put your hands out."

Lowell put his hands in front of him and Jimmy clasped handcuffs on his wrists while the large man kept his gun aimed directly at Vivian.

They drove downtown on the FDR and crossed the Brooklyn Bridge. Lowell tried to keep track of where they were, but he wasn't that familiar with the borough and was soon lost.

They went deeper into Brooklyn, past downtown and up Smith Street. They passed dozens of upscale restaurants and small bodegas. After a while the neighborhood changed, became less residential. They entered a quiet, dimly lit area. The window was down and Lowell could smell the water.

The limo finally pulled up to the warehouse. It was dark, except for a single naked light bulb hanging outside the building. The moon was hidden behind some clouds and the air was thick and still.

The back door opened and the little man Lowell had also encountered in Soho was there holding a gun.

"Get in there." Jimmy pointed to the warehouse door.

Lowell and Vivian entered followed closely by Jimmy and his two henchmen. They walked into the main room. Fat Jimmy was sitting at the table, a half-eaten chicken leg in his hand.

"See Uncle Jimmy, I got 'em."

He finished the leg in one bite and put the bone down. He wiped his hands on a paper napkin, stood up and walked over to them. "You got 'em? After three tries you got 'em."

"Fat Jimmy DeAngelo," said Lowell. "My god, are you involved in this thing?"

"Don't call me that!" He looked closely at Lowell. "I remember you from the floor of the Merc. You're that trader guy, works with the stars."

"Good memory."

"How'd it work out?"

"I bought calls in oil when the futures were trading around thirty-two and kept rolling them over until the top. Then I shorted."

"Wow, must have made a killing. How'd you do it?"

"It was just as Pluto, ruler of oil, entered Sagittarius, the most expansive of signs, and I knew we were in for a sky-rocket ride up."

"I don't know what the hell you're talking about, but good for you. I don't care how you do it, as long as you make money. So now, what the hell are you doing in my business?"

"I'm now a private detective. And I'm working on Freddie Finger's murder."

Jimmy was breathing heavily. He turned to his nephew. "This is the guy you couldn't take care of? This little shrimp?"

"Where did you get these guys?" asked Lowell.

"They're from the old neighborhood."

"But, Uncle Jimmy, you should'a seen him. He was throwing people around like they were dolls. Look what he did to Murray and Leo." He pointed to the large man, his arm still in a sling.

"Murray and Leo?" asked Lowell.

Fat Jimmy shrugged. "I grew up in a Jewish neighborhood."

"Hey, I just wasn't ready for him, that's all," said Murray. "Wait till I get my arm back, then I'll show you. Right, Skinny Jimmy?"

Fat Jimmy saw the smile creeping across Lowell's face. "He's my nephew."

"Fat Jimmy and Skinny Jimmy," said Lowell. "It must have made it easier to fill out seating cards at weddings."

"Yeah, now I remember, you're into that Judo crap. I saw you do a demonstration outside the cotton pit one year. And you got a big mouth, I remember that, too."

"It's aikido, and I remember that day. In fact, I offered to take you on, but you refused."

"I didn't have time to waste wrestling. I was there to make money. While you were throwing people around the room I caught a seventy cent move in silver."

"It's all about the money, isn't it?"

"Well, isn't it?"

"Is that why you killed those rockers?" Lowell was fishing.

Fat Jimmy belched loudly. "Damn, excuse me. It's that acid reflux crap. He took a sip of soda and turned to Lowell. "I didn't kill anyone." Then he looked at his nephew. "Although I might start."

"Jimmy thinks he's the godfather," Lowell said to Vivian. "I used to watch him waddle around the floor of the exchange, clerks and traders kissing his ass."

"If you're trying to piss me off, you're succeeding," said the fat man.

"If you didn't kill them then why are we here?" asked Vivian.

"Because your boyfriend was getting in the way of my business."

"What business is that," Lowell asked.

"Never you mind."

"Jimmy, you're not stupid."

"Hell no, I got a BA from Iona College. I even got credits toward an MBA."

"I'm impressed. Why didn't you complete the degree?"

"I made more money trading commodities the first year I was on the floor than the whole college makes. You don't need a degree to make money."

"Well, you're acting stupid now. Who put you on to me?"

"I don't know. I got a phone call one night telling me that if I wanted my, uh, business to flourish I better get you out of the way. The next day I get a snapshot of you in the mail along with your office address."

"So you sent the boys to take care of me. How thoughtful."

"They were supposed to scare you off the first time. Then they were supposed to grab you and bring you back here so I could talk to you, that's all."

"Ever hear of a phone?"

"I wanted to, you know, make it a little more forceful than just a chat."

"And you don't know who called you or sent the picture?"

"No, but if I knew it was gonna be such a fucking problem I never would have started in the first place. Now I don't know what to do."

"Why don't you just let us go?" asked Vivian.

Jimmy just snorted, then turned to Murray. "You think you can put them in the locker without getting beat up?"

"I think so, Mister Jimmy."

"Well, do it. I need some time to think."

Chapter Thirty

They dumped Andy in a dark alley, his hands and feet tied, and a cloth bag stuck over his head. He was able to get the sack off by pulling his legs up as far as he could, and catching the end of it in his knees. It took half an hour of rubbing the ropes against the ragged, concrete edge of the building, periodically scrapping his flesh as well, but he was finally able to break through. Both his forearms were raw and bleeding. He sat up against the building wall and untied his feet.

He got to the street and looked around. Nothing looked familiar. There was some traffic to the right and he walked toward it. His cell phone and wallet were gone. He always kept a hundred dollar bill in his shoe. Sure enough they had overlooked it. At the corner he stuck out his hand and a cab pulled over.

"Twenty fourth and Park," he told the driver.

"Manhattan?" asked the cabbie.

"Of course. Why, where are we?"

"Off the Grand Concourse, the Bronx."

This was going to be some cab fare.

When he got to the office Andy went up and opened the door with his key. He turned on the light on Sarah's desk and started going through her phone book. Without his cell phone he couldn't remember anyone's number.

He called Sarah and Mort, both of whom arrived in twenty minutes.

"We have to call the police," said Sarah, after she'd cleaned Andy scraps and put some antibiotic ointment and bandages on.

Andy put his shirt back on. "They won't be able to do anything. But at least try and reach Lieutenant Roland and tell him what's happened. Though I doubt that he'll be there at one in the morning."

Sarah picked up the phone and called.

"Nineteenth precinct," said a female voice.

"Lieutenant Roland."

"One moment."

"This is Lieutenant Roland."

"Lieutenant, this is Sarah…"

"…after the beep please record your message." Beeeeeeep!

"Lieutenant, it's Sarah Palmer. David's been kidnapped, and we think they got Vivian Younger, too. Please call me back on my cell phone, 917-555-0312."

"Now what?" said Mort.

"Now," said Andy, "we go find them."

"How?"

"The limo has a tracker."

"I don't think we should go busting in on kidnappers," said Sarah.

Andy thought for a moment. "Well, unless we hear from Roland there isn't much help we could get this late at night. And if we wait until morning it might be too late. Let's at least find them, then we can decide what to do."

They went to the garage in the building's basement where Lowell kept a Mazda. Andy had keys to all of Lowell's vehicles. They quickly piled in with Andy reading the information from the limo's GPS, and headed downtown. They crossed the Brooklyn Bridge, drove up Smith Street through Carroll Gardens, and through the borough down to the waterfront.

Andy stopped the car. "It should be right around here."

There was nothing but a few rundown warehouses and cracking streets with vegetation growing within the crevices, life struggling to survive wherever it can.

"Now what?" asked Mort.

"There's the car." Andy pointed to the warehouse. "I'll bet they're in there." He crept up and looked in the gated window. "They're in there, alright. I recognize one of the guys that jumped me."

"How many are there?" asked Sarah.

"I don't know, I saw about three or four."

"Did you see the boss or Vivian?"

"No. It looks like there's a back room. They must be in there."

"Look," said Sarah, "I've got an idea."

Chapter Thirty-one

Lowell and Vivian were brought into a smaller room and placed in a wire cage about eight feet by ten feet that was used to store valuables. There was a small padlock on the door. The small mean-looking man, Leo, was left to guard them.

"I didn't forget what you did to me last week," he said, once Lowell was safely locked up.

"I hope you didn't. I wouldn't want to have to remind you again."

The little man sneered and walked away.

"What are we going to do now?" asked Vivian.

"Wait and watch."

Leo returned with Fat Jimmy.

"I want to know what you know," said Jimmy.

Lowell smiled. "You couldn't know what I know in a dozen lifetimes."

"Don't get smart with me, Mr. Private Detective, or I'll have Leo splatter your brains all over the lady's pretty dress."

"There's a pleasant thought," said Vivian.

"I'd like that," the little man waved the gun at them. "I'd like that very much."

"Be careful with that thing," said Vivian, "it might go off."

"Yeah, it just might."

"Look," said Lowell, "you're in over your head, Jimmy. About the only chance you have of getting out of this with your ass intact is to let us out of here."

There was a loud banging at the door. "Who the hell would that be? Leo, you and Murray go check it out." He turned to Lowell. "Don't try anything stupid."

Lowell held up his handcuffed wrists. "What am I going to do with these on?"

Leo went to the front door with his gun drawn. "Who's there?"

"Our car broke down and you have the only lights on in the whole neighborhood. Do you think we could use the phone?" asked a female voice.

Leo opened the door a little bit and looked out. He saw a pretty redheaded girl and a skinny, lanky man.

"We don't have a phone."

"You must have a cell phone. Couldn't you just let me use it for a minute? We're lost and it's so late."

"I don't have a cell phone either."

Leo started to close the door. Andy shoved his two hundred thirty pounds against the door pushing Leo onto the floor, his gun spinning across the room. Andy rushed in, his gun drawn, followed by Sarah. While everyone's attention was on them Mort was able to sneak in and scurried unnoticed toward the back of the warehouse. Murray lunged at Andy and grabbed for his gun.

Fat Jimmy fired once into the air. "Everybody freeze." They all stopped in mid-motion. "What have we here? The cavalry to the rescue? Everybody sit against that wall, now!"

They sat.

"Where's my boss?" asked Sarah. "Where are David Lowell and Ms. Younger?"

◇◇◇

Lowell and Vivian had heard the commotion and assumed correctly what was going on. The door to the back room opened slowly. Vivian held her breath.

Mort crept low to the ground and popped his head up in front of the cage.

"Mort," said Lowell, quietly, "am I glad to see you."

"Likewise."

"Can you get us out of here?"

"Piece of cake." He took his tool kit out and removed two long pieces of metal, which he inserted into the lock. In about thirty seconds the cage door was open. Then he took a smaller piece of metal from the kit and started working on the handcuffs. In a few moments they were off.

They crept out of the office and into the main warehouse room. The three crouched down behind some large boxes.

"Now what the fuck am I going to do with all these people?" Fat Jimmy paced back and forth in front of his captives.

"What about the other two in there?" Leo pointed toward the back room.

"Yeah, you might as well get them, too."

Leo walked to the back of the warehouse past the boxes. As he reached for the door Lowell came out from behind and put one hand across his mouth, grabbed the hand holding the gun and quietly disarmed him. Then he twisted the man's neck, knocking him out.

He picked up the gun, jumped out from behind the boxes and pointed it directly at Fat Jimmy. "If anyone moves you get it right between the eyes." He turned to Vivian. "I always wanted to say that line."

"Well, the reading was wonderful. Just a touch of humor with the malice."

"Hey, take it easy, don't anyone do anything stupid."

"Jimmy, you're really starting to piss *me* off," said Lowell, "and I'm done with it. We're taking this whole mess downtown and let the cops sort it out."

"You," he pointed to Murray, "drop your gun and kick it over here."

Murray took his piece out and dropped it on the floor.

"Good," said Lowell, "now kick it over."

Murray did so.

He looked at Skinny Jimmy. "Now you."

Jimmy had his gun out and was about to comply when Leo came barreling out from behind the boxes. His head was twisted in a strange manner.

"Leo, Jesus," said Skinny Jimmy, "what happened to you?"

Leo roared like a crazed lion and charged Lowell, head down. The aikido training had more than prepared Lowell for such an attack, and Leo was soon on the ground once again, holding a sore neck. Skinny Jimmy was nervously holding his gun aimed at Lowell, his hands shaking, and it suddenly went off. As he went down, Leo managed to get a piece of Lowell's shirt and inadvertently pulled him out of the way of the bullet. The shot went past Lowell's head and struck the side of the boiler. The spark it created was just enough to set off the highly flammable packing material lying in a pile. A small flame began unobserved behind the boiler.

"God damn it, Jimmy," said Lowell, "if you do that again I'm going to shoot you. Now put the damn gun down."

Jimmy held it defiantly.

Lowell aimed the gun at a light across the warehouse and took it out without a second glance.

"Damn!" said Sarah, "It thought you didn't know anything about guns."

"I said I didn't like them, not that I couldn't shoot them." His attention returned to Skinny Jimmy. "What's it gonna be, Jimmy?"

"All right." He bent down to put the gun on the floor.

Sarah suddenly yelled: "Fire!"

They looked to the back of the warehouse and saw the flames beginning to grow.

Fat Jimmy was closest to the door. He ran toward it and was the first one out.

Sort of.

They all ran to the sole exit only to find Fat Jimmy stuck in the door jam.

"Get out of the way," they all shouted.

"I can't, I'm stuck."

"You got in here."

"Well, I can't get out."

"It's the fucking chicken legs," said Skinny Jimmy. "I told you that food would kill you, I just didn't plan on going with you."

"Suck in your stomach," said Mort.

"Is he kidding?" asked the fat man.

His nephew and Murray began to pull and tug various parts of the man's body, to no avail.

Lowell looked back at the fire, ever growing. "What's in those crates?"

Fat Jimmy turned his head so he could see. "Propane tanks."

"Are they full?"

The fear in Jimmy's face told Lowell what he needed to know. "The windows are all gated, no fire escape or hidden passages you guys built?"

"What is this, the Great Escape?" answered Fat Jimmy. "It's a freakin' warehouse down by the docks."

"We have to ram him through," said Lowell.

Andy and Murray started from a good twenty feet back. They both got a running start and *BAM!* They slammed into Fat Jimmy simultaneously using their shoulders.

"I think we moved him," said Murray.

"Cut it out!" shouted Jimmy. "You're killing me."

"We haven't got much time left," said Lowell. "You better get him out this time."

On the second try they did manage to eject him out of the doorway. He rolled onto the sidewalk and slowly got to his feet. The rest all ran from the warehouse.

Fat Jimmy's limousine was parked about ten feet from the building right next to Lowell's. Jimmy took his nephew's arm and walked nonchalantly to the car and opened the back door. Leo got behind the wheel and Murray got in the passenger's seat in front.

"Floor it," Jimmy told Leo, once they were in. The limo peeled out.

Andy jumped into Lowell's limo and spun the car around. Lowell, Sarah, Mort, and Vivian got in the back. "Boss?"

"Follow them."

"You got it. Hang on."

As they approached the ramp to the Brooklyn Bridge they heard an explosion and turned to see a gray puff of smoke where the warehouse used to be.

Jimmy saw it too, one more piece of his empire gone.

Sarah's phone rang. "Hello? Oh, Lieutenant…Yes that's right…no I wasn't kidding… Well, he's all right. In fact, he's here. Hold on."

She handed the phone to Lowell.

"We're just about to cross the Brooklyn Bridge in my limo following Fat Jimmy DeAngelo…Yes, he's still alive. He's in a limo too…Yes, he's involved in this mess…All right, we'll see you there."

He hung up.

"Well?" asked Sarah.

"He'll have the cops stop him when he gets into Manhattan."

When they crossed the bridge they saw Jimmy's limo on the right side of the road, several patrol cars surrounding it.

Andy pulled up behind the cop cars and they all got out.

Roland arrived about ten minutes later. He walked over to Lowell.

"Well," said Roland, "what's this all about?"

"It's a long story, Lieutenant. I'll fill you in on the details tomorrow. It's almost four in the morning and we're all very tired."

"Just be at my office by nine."

"Let's say ten."

"Thank god we caught the murderers. I'll schedule a press conference for noon tomorrow." Roland looked sheepishly at Lowell. "And I'll mention how helpful you were in solving the case."

"But I don't know if they killed anyone."

"What do you mean? You said…"

"I said that Jimmy was involved. I just don't know to what extent."

"If he didn't do it, then who did?"

"I don't know if he did or didn't. We'll discuss it all tomorrow at ten."

"Lieutenant," called out one of the policemen, "what should we do?"

Roland turned and saw the problem. They couldn't fit Jimmy into the patrol car. "Ah, hell. You'd better drive him to the precinct in his limo. He won't fit in anything else."

As Fat Jimmy sat in the back of his limo waiting to be driven to police headquarters Lowell walked over shaking his head. "So Jimmy, did you learn anything from all of this?"

He thought for a moment. "Yeah, don't use Jewish gangsters."

Chapter Thirty-two

The next day Lowell picked up Vivian and they went to the precinct. Mort and Sarah were already there and had given statements.

"Hi boss," said Mort.

"Good morning everyone," said Lowell.

"All right, Lowell," said Roland, "what have you got for me? Who killed Freddie? I've got to have something to give the press. If I don't give them a killer, and soon, I may be looking for another job."

"Did you get anything out of DeAngelo?"

"Nah, he swears he had nothing to do with killing them. He made bail this morning, but we'll be all over him from now on. He does have an alibi for the time of Freddie's death."

"You don't really think Fat Jimmy killed him and then strung him up, do you? I doubt that he could lift Freddie. And there's isn't a chair that could hold him as he strung up the body."

"Of course not. But several people, or that big guy, Murray could."

Lowell nodded.

"We're looking into his financial records and the whereabouts of his known associates at the time of Freddie's demise."

"Well, let me know what you find out. I'll follow some other leads."

When they were outside, a town-car pulled up behind Lowell's limo and the driver got out and nodded toward Vivian.

"Sarah, let's go get some shoes." Vivian turned toward Lowell. "See you later?"

"Of course."

◇◇◇

Vivian hired a car and driver whenever she was visiting New York. She always used the same chauffeur, a charming, polite young man named Philip. He drove them to the Village and dropped them off at Broadway and 16th Street.

"How long have you worked for David?"

"A little over three years."

Two Japanese tourists recognized Vivian and snapped their picture. Sarah smiled broadly for the camera.

"How did you two hook up?"

"A friend of mine had been an astrology client of David's for years. When he went into the detective business I was unemployed and my friend recommended me."

"Was it a difficult interview?"

"He asked for my birth information, punched it into his computer and said: *Can you start tomorrow?*"

"He obviously puts a lot of faith in astrology."

"And how." Sarah pushed her bright red hair behind her ears.

They walked through Union Square and bought some muffins and bottles of fresh apple juice from upstate at the farmer's market. Then they crossed Fourteenth Street and walked past University Place.

"Look at all the young people."

"Sure," replied Sarah, "you're in the middle of NYU."

They strolled down Fifth Avenue and Sarah pointed out some of the tiny cobble-stone side alleys left virtually unchanged since the eighteenth century.

"There isn't really a campus, per se, but all these buildings," Sarah waved her hands in a circular motion, "are part of NYU."

It was getting very hot, so they went to Eighth Street and the air conditioning. There were several shoe stores in a row and a few more down the block and across the street. They entered the first and began ogling the merchandise.

"So how is it working for him?" Vivian had a red pump in her hands.

Sarah admired the shoe. "He's not like anyone I've ever known."

"How so?"

"Well, for one thing he's probably the smartest person I've ever met. And maybe the most arrogant."

Vivian bent down and put the red shoe next to Sarah's foot. "You must know him very well."

"I thought I did, until last week." She slipped her foot into the shoe and they both scrutinized it.

"What happened?"

"When we were attacked downtown he threw this big guy around like he weighed nothing. You should have seen it, it was amazing. He called it aikido, said it was a martial art."

"I've heard of it."

"But it wasn't even that, it was the fruit that blew my mind."

"What fruit?"

Sarah told her about Lowell using the melon and nectarines as weapons of convenience.

"So he even has secrets from you?"

"Yeah," Sarah smiled, as she slipped her feet into black heels, "but I know where he keeps them, and I'm gonna get in one day."

"Why *did* he become a detective?"

"He didn't tell you?"

"No, and I'm wrong to ask you. Forget I said anything. I'll find out if and when he chooses to tell me."

They both looked at Sarah's feet in the mirror.

"So are you going to tell me already, or what?"

Sarah nodded. "Of course, it's not much of a secret anyway. You could find all this out on the Internet. About eight years ago, before I came to work for him, David was down on Wall Street making a killing in commodities. He had let his private practice fall apart and was pretty much using astrology just to make money. He apparently made a ton of it, although he won't tell me how much.

"Anyway, there was a holdup in a grocery store and David's son, Robert, was killed. His wife blamed David, said if he had a gift he should have been paying attention to his family and using it to watch over them. Of course he was only working in the financial markets so he *could* watch over them and not have to worry about the financial woes they were having, but she didn't see it that way."

"What happened?"

"She left him."

Vivian's eyes lowered. "But losing a child."

"I know. And he never talks about it."

They were silent for a moment.

"So David became a detective?"

"At first it was to catch his son's killers, which he did. But after that I believe he continued to do it because he has a strong sense of fair play and feels that the world is an unjust place. In his way he likes to feel that he is helping to balance things out."

"He told you this?"

"Nah, I could see it in the cases he chooses to take, and the way he deals with his clients. He only takes the cases where he thinks someone has been wrongfully abused and he believes there is something he can actually do about it."

Vivian looked at Sarah with new admiration. "You're pretty impressive yourself."

Sarah smiled. "I have a few secrets of my own."

"So why did you choose to work for him?"

"I got a degree in social work. If I had taken a job in my chosen profession I would make about thirty grand a year, and be paying off my student loans until I'm ninety."

"He pays you well?"

Sarah winked. "And there's perks," she nodded toward her shoes. "And he has solved every case he has taken."

"So far."

Chapter Thirty-three

The next day Lowell was gazing out the window and petting the turtles when Sarah buzzed. He was stuck, as often happened when Mercury was in retrograde.

"Boss, Roger from Morgan Stanley on line one."

"Roger, thanks for getting back to me. What have you got?"

"Sorry it took so long. We've been having problems with the computers ever since Mercury retrograded. See, and you thought I didn't follow your newsletter. Just give me a minute, let me bring it up. Here it is. In 1997 Prudential Insurance issued a fifty-five million dollar bond with a promise of seven point nine percent return against profits from David Bowie's recordings. It consisted of about twenty-five albums and several hundred songs. I can look it up if you need the exact figures."

"No, I don't think that's necessary."

"Well, the Bowie bond was put together by a fellow named David Pullman, and today these are often called Pullman bonds. After Bowie, a number of other acts including James Brown, Ashford and Simpson, the Isley Brothers and, of course, as I'm sure you knew, Freddie took advantage of the financial climate and had bonds issued against their work as well."

"So what happened? How did the bonds do?"

"Quite well for the first few years. The bond paid its eight percent return, and there was a big bonus for the underwriters. But after a while things started to turn bad."

"How so?"

"As you know, album sales tanked in the late nineties. CDs had propped things up for a good while, as boomers rushed to replace all their vinyl. But that peaked, and then in a classic case of unintended consequences, the digitization that created the CD also created the means to download just the good tracks. The one-two punch of the iPod, and free music on the Internet starting with Napster, plunged the record industry into very hard times. And musicians and their work lost a lot of their revenue-making power."

"What happened to the bonds?"

"A number of years ago Moody's lowered the rating on Bowie's bond from A3 to BBB3, one level above junk bonds. I assume the same was done to the other Pullman bonds issued as well. For several years the return was lowered, and some investors began to complain, although none actually defaulted. There were no more underwriters, and no more bonds issued. Freddie's was one of the last. Recently there has been a bit of interest shown again because of the success of iTunes and several other legal online music sources. But I doubt you will see the kind of revenue these guys made anytime in the near future. The music business is changing, and the hey-day of the seventies, eighties, and nineties is long gone."

"But people still get rich in the music business?"

"Oh sure, some make a fortune," replied Roger. "But not as many as used to. And the catalogues of the old acts aren't worth anything near what they were."

"Who issued the bond for Freddie?"

"Goldman Sachs. They issued shares to individual investors."

"Do you know who bought the lion's share?"

"No, but I'll try to find out for you."

"Keep an eye out and let me know if Jimmy DeAngelo's name shows up."

"Fat Jimmy from the floor of the Merc?"

"The same."

"Okay. What do you think of the markets?"

"I think the stocks are still much too risky for a long term position. As long as this Uranus – Pluto square continues they will have violent ups and downs. You're better off playing the volatility. I would stay liquid, and look for oversold commodities. We could see shortages in some soon. I'm still long oil, as well as wheat, soybeans, and the other agriculturals. And watch the Pound. Mars is about to enter Virgo and it should make a correction. Thanks, Roger. You've been a big help."

After they hung up Lowell made a note of his conversation and left it on Mort's desk.

Chapter Thirty-four

They sat around the big circular table in the back of First Wok on Third Avenue and 88th Street. It was four-thirty in the afternoon, and the restaurant was empty except for their party. Outside, rush hour traffic was just beginning to clog the avenue.

Nine of the chairs were filled. The tenth was left empty.

The waiter took their drink order, seven sodas and two teas. When the drinks arrived Marty stood up holding his ginger ale. "Before we go any further," he faced the empty chair, "a toast to Bill "The Walrus" Martin, one of the greatest bass players this city and rock n' roll ever knew." Billy had been gunned down in the subway on his way home from a gig late one night about ten years earlier.

"To Billy," said a few.

"You all know why we're here," Marty looked over the faces of his old comrades.

"You're sure you want to do this?" asked J. R.

Marty looked at him. "You're the best damned guitarist and engineer I ever worked with. You worked on over a hundred albums?"

"Over two hundred."

"You had some pretty good years, didn't you? Probably made a couple hundred thou per? How much you got left?"

"I was divorced twice, you know."

"What did you make last year? Thirty grand? We can't even make a living in New York anymore. There used to be dozens of top notch piano rooms in this city. Now there's about five. An Italian restaurant on Lexington was looking for a pianist-singer a few months ago. I went there and auditioned. The guy almost dropped his teeth when he heard me. Then he offered me a hundred dollars a night for five hours. That's what they paid me in 1976 when I first came to New York. I told him I couldn't afford to work there. I thought about following the pianist from the Carlyle and pushing him down the subway stairs, then running to audition." There was a little nervous laughter at the table. "I'm kidding, of course."

"There used to be so much work, commercials, records to cut, and live gigs everywhere. It started getting bad with digital," said Steve Whoo, a great drummer who had also played on hundreds of top selling albums.

"At least they made your song, "You Wiped Me Out," into a commercial last year," said Mark Lineberry, guitarist, producer, and genius.

"Yeah, for a debt consolidation company."

"It could have been worse. It could have been for toilet paper."

They all laughed.

"What did you do with the money?"

"I paid off my debts."

The waiter came over. They ordered a load of different appetizers.

"Well, here's to the old days when most of us would have been carried out of here at the end of the evening." Mark took another sip of soda. "Ah, that's delicious."

Most of them had been in AA or drug rehab.

"Um, any of you still, uh, you know," said Marty, miming a smoke.

"Sure."

"You bet."

"Of course, I wouldn't give *that* up."

"*That's* not drugs."

They went out three at a time and each took a few tokes. By the time the last group came back the food had arrived. Most of them dove in with great zeal.

"So, how are you guys?" asked Marty, a dumpling heading toward his mouth. Many hadn't seen each other in years.

"I'm fine," said J. R. "My PSA is a little high."

"Yeah?" said Richard, "mine too. How high is yours?"

"About seven and change."

"Mine's over nine. But they say it's not the number but how much it changes."

"Have you tried Saw Palmetto? It's wonderful. I use a combination of that and pygeum. It works wonders."

"Stop it," said Steve. "Listen to us. We're talking like little old men. Girls used to drool when we entered a club."

"Now we do," said Lineberry.

"Age is all in your head," said J. R.

"Tell that to my prostate," added Richard.

"It's not just the business that's changed," said J. R. "This city has gone to hell in a hand basket. They've made it impossible to live here. I've got less than two years left on the lease at my recording studio in the west thirties. If the landlord pigs out on me I'm done. The only way I stayed in business this long is that I came in on a sweetheart deal during the seventies when nobody wanted to live here. But my wife has a good job with a pension and we got a small place upstate, so I guess we'll be okay."

"I got a house near Nashville that I bought for a hundred thousand when *Squeeze Toy* was on the charts," said Richard. "I might just move there permanently. Marty, why don't you come down to Nashville? I can get you some work playing keyboards. Maybe you can sell a song or two. What do you say?"

"I'll talk it over with Beth."

"We may be the last generation of homegrown New York artists," said Walter. "Will there ever be another Tin Pan Alley, a Village folk or jazz renaissance? I've always liked to teach, and I've seen a change in the past ten years. Young musicians aren't flocking to this city the way we did. They don't want to work forty hours a week just to pay the rent on a tiny little hole in the wall and put together a band. It isn't worth it to them. This city doesn't have a thriving, boiling underground like it used to."

"No Lou Reed, Patty Smith, or Dylan coming from these kids, huh?" said Steve.

"No, it'll be the Internet where new heroes will be found. Hyperspace nightclubs."

"Isn't that a shame," said Walter. "There were so many places to play in New York in the seventies and eighties, and everybody went out to hear live music. On the Upper East Side alone there was J.P.'s, Eric's, Friends, Dr. Generosity's, Home Bar, it was wonderful. The record executives would hop from bar to bar and check out the live acts. Nobody could open a new club uptown now. The rent would make it impossible."

J. R. got a faraway look in his eyes. "Remember when James Taylor would come up after the band had cleared the equipment off the stage at J.P.'s and sing until four in the morning?"

"I was in Home Bar on Second Avenue once in the eighties," said Marty. "I came to listen to a band called Elephant's Memory. I was loaded when I got there and sat next to an Englishman and chatted for hours about all kinds of things. He was there to consider the group for his back-up band. The next day I went in, a bit hung over, and Jimmy, the bartender asked if I had had a good time the night before. I told him, *Yes, I had a great time chatting with some very nice Englishman who had come to hear the band. Yes,* said the bartender, *that very nice Englishman was John Lennon.*"

They all laughed uproariously.

"Elephant's Memory became the Plastic Ono Band," said J. R."

"That's right," said Walter.

"God, I miss those days," said Marty. "Just to get together and play the blues and some old rock 'n roll."

"Why don't you come down to B. B. King's next week," said Steve. "Every Monday night they run an informal jam downstairs, mostly blues and old rock tunes."

"You know, I'd love to. It's been years since I just played for fun."

"That's the only thing they can't take away from us."

"Now, here's the question we ask every ten years or so," said J. R. "How many of you were at Woodstock?" Eight including Marty raised their hands. "Now, how many were *really* at Woodstock?"

Four of them lowered their hands. Marty's stayed up.

"So, the truth will out."

Marty smiled. "You know who I went with?"

"Who?"

"Freddie."

"You're kidding. Really?"

"He got his father's station wagon and about seven of us piled in."

"So," said Walter, "you hung out with Freddie Finger at Woodstock."

"Not really. The minute we got out of the car he dumped me and disappeared into a sea of humanity. I never saw him again until we were back in Westchester."

"How'd you get home?"

"It was Woodstock. Everybody offered me a ride."

"Everybody except Freddie," said Steve.

"Alright," continued Marty, "now down to business."

Chapter Thirty-five

The next morning Lowell was about to begin his day's work when Melinda came in carrying two deli coffee cups.

"Hi, dad, I've got a meeting near here in an hour. Thought I'd stop by to say hello. Hope you don't mind?" She handed Lowell one of the coffees.

"Not at all. I'm delighted to see you. I was just about to begin the examination of the relationship charts." He pointed to the pile of papers he had accrued. "These are all the suspects, but none showed the transits or progressions one would associate with a murder."

"Nobody stands out?"

"There are plenty of natal charts that displayed enough anger or explosiveness necessary for an act of violence. Marty Winebeck has a Mars – Uranus square. Several of the Rocket Fire members also showed a propensity toward anger and frustration. Even Tracy's birth chart has a Sun-Uranus conjunct, showing an inner stress that could easily come out in an act of sudden violence."

"I thought she was calm and a little dumb, the way you described her?"

"Libras are very good at hiding their animosity. They tend to be passive-aggressive, but do manage to get what they want, mostly by circumventing the situation and working behind the scenes, rather than direct confrontation. But if someone is going to commit premeditated murder, and Freddie's death certainly was that, certain planetary configurations should show up actively in the transits, secondary progressions, and solar arc directed charts. One would expect to see Mars, the god of war, and Pluto, planet of vengeance and hidden agendas, involved. Also, more likely than not, Uranus, the planet of sudden and explosive events would also make a prominent appearance. It was also possible that Saturn, the planet of restriction and frustration, could be sufficiently active to force an event. In other words, there is any number of combinations that *could* conceivably create the atmosphere conducive to a murder.

"But the problem with this case is that the most prominent planet is Neptune. In the natal charts of most of the suspects overwhelming presence makes this a difficult and confusing situation. Neptune, as you know, rules music and the arts in general, so one would expect it to be active in the charts of musicians and other artists. But it isn't by nature a violent or aggressive energy. In fact, it's just the opposite. It can be overly passive, and it's often difficult to act in a decisive way when this planet is around. So the answer must lie in the composite charts."

"Okay, tell me about the composites."

"The band members' charts are particularly interesting." He tugged on his ponytail. "Remember, anyone is capable of murder under the right circumstances. But planning and carrying this kind of action would take a certain type of personality, or, as I now believe, a group personality. I don't believe any of these people has it in their natal charts to do away with the three victims alone. But there are several combinations that could be sufficient to create a composite murderer. If you add the charts of the drummer and guitarist, for example, as a team they are far more aggressive and controlling than as individuals."

"Did they do it?"

"I don't know yet. I'll have to examine many more charts before I can see. It may just be that as individuals they would never have had enough ego to make it in the business. But working together they strengthened and supported each other sufficiently for success. It doesn't mean they are murderers."

"What about the managers?"

"Larry Latner's chart shows a weak, small-minded character. Not terribly bright, but with a strong sense of self-preservation. It's not that powerful a chart. Gleason's and Frey's both show a lot of business savvy but not a lot of will. I'll do the composites between the three managers and see what I come up with."

He rubbed his eyes. "Then there's the added pleasure of Fat Jimmy DeAngelo's gang."

Melinda took a sip of her coffee. "Isn't Jimmy DeAngelo that really overweight guy you told me about from the commodities exchange?"

"The same."

"He must have some chart."

"What would you expect?"

"I guess he has an afflicted ascendant."

"Right. The ascendant rules the physical body, so weighing around four hundred pounds, what planet would you expect to see in such an unusual case?"

"Uranus?"

"Besides being an Aquarius, which is ruled by that planet, Jimmy does have Uranus conjunct his ascendant, which guarantees some unusual physical situation. Excellent. But he could be very tall, or very short, very thin, or very strange in some way. Why would he be exceedingly large?"

The student thought for a moment. "Jupiter!"

"Exactly! You always were my prize student. Jimmy has Jupiter conjunct Uranus on the ascendant. That would imply an unusual and very large physical body."

"But couldn't he have been seven feet tall. So why did it result in excessive weight?"

"Here's the chart." Lowell handed her the paper. "He was born February 12th, 1955, at 2:49 p.m. in New York City."

She studied it for a few moments. "I guess if Jupiter and Uranus were conjunct in a fire sign on the ascendant, he would have been very tall. But the Cancer rising sign tends to be a bit heavy to begin with, and so his body took on the natural

Cancerian propensity toward weight and the Jupiter exaggerated it."

"You really are good, you know? And Mars squares the Jupiter, Uranus, Ascendant conjunction, so?"

"He's angry about it."

"Very. Jimmy has the Sun conjunct Mercury in Aquarius, so he's actually really quite bright. It is inconjunct those Cancer planets, and the Sun and Mercury square Saturn, so things aren't easy for him. He's lonely and socially inept. He's also more concerned with accruing money and power than doing anything constructive with it. The Sun and Mercury also oppose Pluto, so Jimmy is a very frustrated and angry man capable of harsh vengeance. He works behind the scenes and is very much a control freak. If he doesn't change his attitude, the afflicted Sun, which rules the heart and circulatory system, will most likely result in a fatal heart attack."

"Did he have Freddie killed?"

"He may be capable of it. I'm not sure yet."

They sat silently for a few moments while Lowell shuffled papers.

"So, you've been spending a lot of time with Vivian Younger?"

He ignored her.

"My god, you're blushing. Dad! You're having an affair with her, aren't you?"

"What? That's nonsense." He turned away.

Melinda laughed. "Why, I think that's wonderful."

"I don't want to talk about it." He picked up a dozen or so charts and began to scrutinize them."

"Well, I'd love to meet her."

Lowell sighed and looked at his daughter. "Do you think we could keep this between us?"

Chapter Thirty-six

It was noon the next day when Sarah buzzed. "It's Roger, from Morgan Stanley."

"Hello, Roger, what have you got for me?"

"When Freddie's bond was issued, most of the people in his life took shares. Some for a few bucks, others for much more. Two of his wives are heavily vested. The majority of shares in Freddie's bond were bought by Brewster, Warren, and Springfield. I tried to find out something about them. But there's nothing.

"You mean they're not that big a firm?"

"I mean there *is* no firm. There is no office, no secretary, no history that I can find at all, only a PO Box."

"How can that be?"

"The bond was issued by Goldman Sachs, who, by the way, also issued the bonds for Redfish and Gene. But anyone can buy a piece of it if they have the money. You don't have to work on Wall Street."

"Can you find out if Brewster, Warren, and Springfield also bought the bonds that Gene and Redfish took out?"

"That I can do. Jimmy DeAngelo's name did show up, as a partner in a holding company that has about three million invested in Freddie's bond, which, by the way, expires in March of next year. In fact, all three do."

"What do you mean?"

"They were all limited issues. After the time limit, the publishing rights revert back to the original copyright owners."

"So I assume that this new album from Rocket Fire will inflate the value of the note."

"Not at all. These bonds only involved the pre-existing catalogue. That's true of all the Bowie bonds. None of Freddie's work from the time the bond was issued on, including the new record, was part of the deal."

"Do you mean to tell me that someone was willing to put up fifty million dollars just for the band's old work? And none of these bonds included anything new to be recorded?"

"That's right," said Roger. "It was all about the old material."

"Well, thanks Roger, I owe you one."

"Come downtown sometime and you can buy me lunch."

◇ ◇ ◇

It was late in the afternoon. Mort came into Lowell's office and walked over to the refrigerator. He took out a Coke and popped the can, taking a healthy swig. He started singing a song under his breath.

"What are you singing?"

"Huh? Oh, I didn't realize I was singing out loud. It's one of Rocket Fire's old hits. I heard it on the radio this morning."

"Well, cut it out, I can't hear myself think."

"Sorry, boss. But that's all you hear on the radio now. Freddie, and Wally, and Gene, that's all anyone is playing."

"Yeah, people get very nostalgic for you when you're dead. And they all just put out new albums, didn't they? So obviously they're going to get played a lot. Can we get back to work now?"

"Actually, no. The release of the new albums by each of the three has been delayed, and all that's getting played is the old albums. It's great to hear them again on the radio."

"I thought they each had an album about to be released."

"They did. But I read in *Rolling Stone* that there were technical difficulties and they all had to be postponed."

"And now everyone is playing their old music?"

Mort nodded. "Yeah. Everybody's doing memorial shows and I heard that they're putting out a "best of" album of each artist as well as a group of younger artists getting together to record their songs. It happens all the time, especially when someone dies."

Lowell picked up the phone and punched in some numbers.

◇◇◇

The second time he came to Latner's office on West 76th Street, Lowell was less impressed. For some reason the house didn't look so formidable. He noticed some structural decay at the base of the building and in between the stones on the walls, which he hadn't seen the first time. The same blond answered the door. She didn't seem so tall this time. Lowell laughed to himself. *I really am a snob.*

"Oh, Mr. Lowell," said, "how nice to see you again so soon. Won't you please come this way?"

Oh, the retorts that came to his mind. But he wasn't in a funny mood. He sat in the waiting room for only a few moments when the blond returned and escorted him into Latner's office.

He stood and extended his hand. "Mr. Lowell, how nice of you to drop by again so soon."

Lowell reluctantly shook the damp hand and then sat.

"What brings you back to my neck of the woods?" Latner took a handful of M&Ms and threw them into his mouth.

"The Bowie Bonds."

If Lowell expected a reaction he was disappointed. Latner sat back and put his hands behind his head.

"Now, what's this all about?"

"When I was here last week you led me to believe that the bond Freddie had taken out was 'as good as gold,' I believe is the term you used."

"And it is. After our chat, I called Goldman Sachs and checked. This quarter it's paying a dividend above the interest rate."

"But that's only because Freddie's dead and every radio station is playing his music. The bond didn't pay the full interest for the last twelve quarters and was about to default."

"I'm sure it's doing better since Freddie's demise." Latner played with the M&Ms, but resisted temptation. "I can't help it if death is a big seller in America. But I don't follow what those bonds are doing. I've got my hands full just managing the business. You know more about them than I do. I just assumed they were doing well all along."

"Why did you decide to hold back the release of Rocket Fire's new album? And why were Redfish's and Gene's records held back as well?"

"I talked it over with Gene's and Redfish's managers and we mutually decided not to flood the markets with too much new material at once, or to complete with each other."

"Business as usual, huh?"

"It is a business, and I have to keep running it. If I can guarantee an increase of several million copies sold by waiting a few weeks, why shouldn't I? If we all released new albums the same month people wouldn't have enough money to buy them all. So we decided to space them out one a month for three months, starting in September. It was just a smart business decision."

He succumbed to his addiction and threw a handful of the bite sized goodies in his mouth. "By waiting it adds to the suspense and builds momentum. It's the same in the movie business, the book business, hell every business. What do they do when they have a new computer game? They talk about it in the press for months, then they release it at midnight on a Friday and everybody goes nuts to own one. That's what we've decided to do."

"The fact that the decision is good for the bonds doesn't enter into it?"

"Not in the slightest. Why would it?"

"You aren't invested in the bond Freddie took out?"

"Oh sure I am. I have a small piece of it, taken out of good faith, but it doesn't amount to much. Everyone in the organization took shares in the bond. The band-members, the roadies, hell even his wives own a piece. Look it up, it's all accessible to the public. But you're not getting the big picture here," he said, condescendingly. "We're talking about tens of millions of dollars, if things are marketed correctly. Maybe that's not a lot of money to you but believe me, the band could use it. This may be the last chance for them to make some real money. They're not kids anymore and there's really no future for them."

"You wouldn't make out too badly either, would you?"

"No, I guess I wouldn't do too badly. But like I told you, I don't really need it."

"Yes, so you've told me."

"Was there anything else? You'll forgive me, but we're extremely busy around here and time is the most precious of all commodities, don't you think?" He extended his hand.

Lowell got up and shook the damp, limp offering and left.

Chapter Thirty-seven

Mort was inhaling a cup of coffee. Lowell was walking back and forth in front of the window. Buster and Keaton were pacing as well, although at an almost imperceptible velocity.

"Mort, I want you to dig into these bonds. Tell me who owns them, how much they've invested, and what shape their finances are in."

He took the work into his office. An hour later he dropped a few pages on Lowell's desk. "Like Latner said, almost everyone who knew Freddie had a piece of his bond. Two of his wives own about a quarter of a million each, Jimmy DeAngelo is in for about three million on Freddie's and about the same on the other two dead rockers, for a total of almost ten million. The band members also own pieces, although not as large. And Latner holds about a hundred grand."

"Did you get anywhere with Brewster, Warren, and Spring-field?"

"Not yet."

"Keep trying. They've got to be somewhere."

"Are you getting anything from the composite charts?"

"I'm focusing on the band and the managers for now. Some of the combinations are very volatile, and I'm hoping that one will jump out. Wives two and three are certainly an interesting pair. Cross referencing relationship charts is a time consuming affair. And my printer is working overtime."

Roland called twice that day.

Melinda came in about two. "How's it going?" Her father's harried face was answer enough.

"I know I'm close. There are several combinations that may be possible. Gene's chart does not show the same violent aspects as the other two. Maybe they weren't all killed for the same reason after all. I'm trying to see this thing from a new perspective now that Mercury is about to change direction once again."

"How?"

"Well, let's say two members of the band did it without the others' knowledge, I must find that combination and remove all others. Once I add a third person that was not part of the equation, it doesn't add up."

"Well, I hope you finish soon. You're starting to look a little weary."

"It's been a trying few weeks. I'll be glad when this case is behind me."

◇◇◇

It took another day and a half of comparing, cross-referencing, and scrutinizing, but Lowell finally had the composite chart he sought. He had been right. There was something so incongruous in the mix it's no wonder it took him so long.

◇◇◇

It was late afternoon when Sarah and Vivian entered the office. Lowell was deep in thought and making calculations on his iPad. Mort was at the second desk working on a computer screen.

"I don't want to bother you," said Vivian, when she saw him. "You seem quite involved."

Lowell raised his head. "Huh? Oh hello ladies. What? No, you're not bothering me."

"It's done anyway," said Mort, before Lowell could stop him.

"What is?" asked Vivian.

"The case. He's solved it."

Lowell's head twitched.

This was the moment he had dreaded from the beginning. Until now she had been running on adrenaline, the anticipation of discovery distracting her from the truth. Her father was dead. And now she was about to find out who was responsible. There would be no more distractions.

"It's not conclusive."

"But Mort just said…"

"What he meant was that the solution was imminent. I'll let you know soon, I promise."

Sarah looked at Mort.

"Mort?"

"I've got to go." He literally ran from the room.

"David, if you know who killed my father, you've got to tell me."

Lowell leaned back in his chair and pulled on his ponytail. "Give me another day, maybe just a few more hours and I'll tell you everything, I promise."

"If you know now why won't you tell me?"

"I'm not one hundred percent sure, and I've got to be very careful or we could tip them off and lose them."

"Don't leave me out of the loop. Don't forget, I'm the reason you're in this to begin with."

He couldn't say that he was only trying to protect her. That would offend her. If his suspicions were right a lot of people would be hurt. And besides, he had to be absolutely sure. If he was wrong he certainly didn't want to make any accusations in public. It was better to confront it behind closed doors.

"I'll tell you what I learn when I return, I promise. I have to do this alone. I'm very sorry."

It was time.

He walked out the front door and turned left toward the elevators. Vivian counted to ten, and then ran out the door to the right and down the stairs.

Andy was waiting by the curb. Lowell got into the limo and they took off.

Chapter Thirty-eight

Andy pulled the limo up to the curb. Lowell opened the back door and got out.

"Stay here," he told the driver. "If I'm not out in twenty minutes make the call." He had a deal with Roland and didn't want to renege on it, but he couldn't resist the drama of this first confrontation. And he had to be absolutely sure.

He was about to go into the building when Vivian jumped from a cab. "What are you doing here?"

Lowell said nothing.

"Oh my god! Here? If you're going to face my father's killer I want to be there."

"My first concern is your safety. I told you that I would keep you informed as the case went on, and I have done so."

"Except when it mattered." She was angry. "How long have you known?"

"I just realized it late last night. And I didn't want to tell you until I was sure."

"And now you are?"

"No, not one hundred percent. Something still doesn't make sense."

"Then let's go find out."

"Vivian, this isn't going to be pleasant."

"Do you think anything about my father's death has been?"

"But the truth…"

"Whatever the truth is," she said with determination, "I want to know it."

Lowell looked over at Andy, who stood leaning against the car, his arms folded across his chest. The driver shrugged when he saw the look, and then put his hand up to his face to mimic a phone call. Lowell nodded.

"Alright, as long as you're here you might as well come with me."

The front door was unlocked and they brazenly entered the building. Nobody was in the outer office, and they walked into the back. There they were, sitting around a table, the co-conspirators, all present, deep in conversation. They didn't even notice their new arrivals.

Lowell coughed.

Everybody stopped what they were doing and turned.

"Well," said the detective, "what have we here?"

"You have no right being here. Get out before I call the police."

"You do that," said Lowell, "and tell them that you are calling from the firm of Warren, Brewster, and Springfield."

"He knows," said one of them.

"Shut up," said the first. "He doesn't know anything, just let me handle this. Mr. Lowell, you are trespassing and seem to be making some sort of accusation."

Lowell put his hands on the back of the only empty chair and looked out at his audience. "Warren, Brewster, and Springfield. Or should I say, Larry Latner, Johnny Gleason, and Richard Frey."

Vivian looked confused. "What's this all about?"

"They took the names of the towns where they grew up for the name of their financial shell company. Larry Latner was raised in Brewster, New York, James Gleason in Warren, Michigan, and Richard Frey in Springfield, Massachusetts. Unfortunately they weren't born in those cities or I would have discovered their connection as soon as I got their birth information. My guess is they've been friends for years. When did you meet, in Harvard?" The guy in the crimson sweatshirt finally made sense.

"Yeah," said Frey, "in the seventies."

"I'm sure your alma mater will be very proud. I assume you anonymously bought the lion's share of your clients' bonds for millions of dollars and figured you'd clean up on it. Isn't that about right?"

The three sat quietly.

"Then you sold off pieces to other investors through a third party, including a very angry Jimmy DeAngelo, to protect part of your investment. When the bonds were about to fail you realized that the only way to save your asses was to kill your own clients. This is a nice business you're in."

"Jesus Christ," said Vivian.

"That's not the way it was." Frey was practically hysterical. "Sure we bought the bonds, there's nothing wrong with that. But Gene's death was an accident, I swear."

Lowell tugged on his ponytail. "Tell me about it."

"We were in New York to promote a new video. The bonds were killing us. We were spending a fortune just to pay dividends to the investors and prevent a total default, or worse. Some of the people we sold shares to weren't going to accept us defaulting. Our lives were in danger."

"So what happened?" asked Lowell.

"One night I admitted to Gene that it was us who had put up the money for the three bonds and begged him to help us out by promoting the old catalogue. He became furious and called me a crook, me! The one who had stood by his side when his records failed in the nineties and stayed loyal to him when his drinking threatened his career. I wasn't a crook."

"And then?" prodded Lowell.

"We were in the hotel and he went crazy. I had never seen him that way. He said he was going to call Freddie and Wally and tell them what was happening and then call the newspapers and tell them he had fired me. He walked over to the phone and, I swear to god, tripped over the damned wire and fell out of the fifteenth story window. On my mother's grave it was an accident."

That's what threw me when I looked at the victim's death charts, thought the astrologer. *Gene's never did match the other two for violence and vengeance. Also Frey's composite chart with the other mangers doesn't add up to murder. He probably was telling the truth.*

"So why didn't you call the police?"

"And tell them what? That Gene was going to fire me and accidentally fell out of the window just before he could expose me? Would you have believed me?"

"So what *did* you do?" asked Lowell.

"I called him," he pointed to Latner.

"Then what? Larry here must have realized the potential, and you all decided to just keep your mouths shut and see what happened? When you saw the enormous increase in air play and record sales for Gene's old catalogue, you knew you'd hit the mother lode." He looked at Latner. "Is that when you decided to kill the other two?"

Frey looked at Latner. "You told me it was probably a rabid fan that killed them? What's the truth?"

Latner shook his head. "I didn't kill anyone."

Frey was frantic. "I was in Boston when Wally and Freddie were killed and I can prove it."

Latner started to pace. "Sure, we were in financial trouble. Vivian, you've got to understand how it was. It was all going to shit. We put up *over one hundred million dollars* and they just pissed it away. And we were going to wind up holding the bag. I was ruined. I don't own a piece of property that isn't mortgaged because of these bonds. If we didn't start getting a return on our investment they were going to expire and we would have to eat it all."

"And the only way out that you could think of was to kill my father?"

"I told you, I didn't kill anyone. I talked to him. I tried to reason with him, begged him to help out in some way. If he had just put out another album of greatest hits we could have made some of it back at least. I asked him to buy back a piece of the bond. He laughed in my face, said if I was stupid enough to give him all that money against old songs I got what I deserved."

Vivian was pale. She looked at Latner. "It was you, wasn't it? Why don't you just admit it? You killed my father."

"He can't admit it," said Lowell. "He's facing twenty-five years to life."

Her eyes flared as she started toward Latner, her hands reaching for him. Lowell stood between them, took her gently, but firmly by the shoulders, and sat her down. She panted audibly. "How could you?"

They were all silent for a moment.

"Besides," added Latner, "he would have loved this."

"Loved what?" asked Vivian. "Being murdered so you could make more money? Is that what he would have loved?"

"You didn't know your father at all. You want to know what he was most afraid of? It wasn't illness or even death. His greatest fear was that he would outlive his fame and nobody would remember him. That his funeral would be playing to an empty house. They were all like that, all the rock stars, narcissists every one. At least he went out in his glory on the very top of the charts. Not only is his new album going to be number one with a bullet but five of his old albums are now on the charts and climbing. There's going to be a massive resurgence of Freddie's music and a whole new generation will know who he was and remember his songs."

Vivian was near tears. "My father looked up to you. He always told me that you were the only one who really cared about the band. The rest were just using them. I...I've known you since I was a little girl. How could you do it? You were a rich man. Why would you have risked it all?"

"Rich? I wasn't rich. I owned some property and had a few bucks in the bank, but I needed that money to get out, get a ranch somewhere. The record business is dying. The Internet killed the whole damn industry years ago. They pay you sixty nine cents and download your hit song, then they send it to everyone they know for free."

She stared at him disbelieving. "You're sick."

"I'm sick? Let me tell you about your dear departed father."

"Latner!" admonished Lowell.

"She wants to judge me, well let her have all the facts." He got up from his chair and started to pace. "Your father was a pig."

"That's enough," Lowell moved a step toward him.

Latner took out a pistol from the desk drawer and pointed it directly at Lowell. "Sit down and listen.

"I nursed that band through drugs and alcohol, pregnant groupies and lousy records. I bailed them out of jail more than once and paid off god knows how many reporters to keep things out of the papers." He turned to Lowell. "You brought up Marty Winebeck a few weeks ago. You want to know what *that* cost to cover up."

"And you didn't give Marty a dime of it."

"It was the principle of the thing. If Freddie paid him off he left himself open to lawsuits and harassment forever."

Lowell shook his head. "So instead you paid off some cops and probably a judge or two and got the whole thing squashed. You could have paid Marty a tenth of what it cost and done the right thing."

"It wasn't as much as you think. Buffalo's a small town. But like I said, it was the principle of the thing."

"You three owned the townhouse we found Freddie in, didn't you?"

"Yeah," said Frey. "We had to sell it to make good on that damned bond." He stared at Latner. "So that's why they found Freddie there. You said it was someone who found out about the bonds and wanted to send us a message. It was you that was sending the message, wasn't it?"

Latner turned back to Vivian. "I protected your father every day of his life for almost forty years. And you know how he repays me? One night I came home to my house in Mount Kisco unexpectedly and saw him through the window prancing around naked. I stayed in the shadows and watched, expecting to see my wife join him. I knew he had been screwing her for years. I didn't mind so much. I just pretended I didn't know. But when my seventeen-year old daughter came out of the room naked, I had had enough."

"So you killed him," said Vivian.

Latner looked at her and shook his head. "It's a dirty world. People have polluted the planet and their souls. You can't turn on the TV or pick up a newspaper without seeing the disgust and contamination all around us. What I saw in my lifetime hanging around these self-proclaimed gods, these abusers of the flesh, was enough to sicken Caligula. I watched little girls by the hundreds take drugs and let them do things to their bodies I wouldn't even talk about. And they thought it was funny. Every one of those girls was somebody's daughter.

"There was only one thing pure and uncontaminated in my world, my little girl, Ashley. And he took that from me after all I had done for him." He shook his head slightly and regained his composure. "I…Whoever killed him did the world a favor. Besides, you can't prove anything."

Lowell tugged on his ponytail. "You must have waited until Freddie left the house and then followed him into the city, sneaked into Cantaloupe's Bar, and put a knockout drug in his soda. And then you put him in a car and took him somewhere and killed him. And you decided to leave him in the townhouse you had to sell to help pay off the bond. You probably thought the police would be too busy to follow the threads and figure this out. And when I was called into the case you put Jimmy DeAngelo on my tail."

"She's a seventeen-year-old girl, for god's sake. He was sixty-three years old, a dirty old man, and he got what he deserved."

Vivian put her face in her hands and wept.

Chapter Thirty-nine

"Now everybody just sit tight," said Latner.

"Where do you think we're going to go?" asked Frey. "You don't think he came here alone, do you?" He picked up the phone.

"What are you doing?"

"I'm calling my lawyer."

Latner pointed the gun at Frey. "Put down that phone."

Frey hung up. "Are you going to kill me, too?"

"Just sit down."

Lowell shook his head. "Latner, it's over."

"Over?" he looked around his office at the gold and platinum records hanging on the walls. "It can't be over." He shook his head. "Do you know how amazing they were, how beautiful rock and roll was, how beautiful Freddie was? When he was young he would strut across the stage like Jaggar, only with a better voice. Their songs were incredible, one hit after another rising to the top ten. For decades everything was going along fine, until that damn Internet ate the fucking record industry in one gulp. And now it's doing it to books, and movies, and all the arts." Rage filled his eyes. "Do you want to know who killed Freddie? I'll tell you."

His hands shook with anger as he aimed the gun at his computer screen. "It was the beast that killed beauty!"

He pulled the trigger. The computer screen shattered into a million pieces, shards of glass flew everywhere. Lowell instinctively covered Vivian with his body.

"You've got nothing on any of us."

"So if you had nothing to do with Freddie's murder," said Lowell, "why don't you just come along with me and we'll sort it all out at the police station?"

Latner turned to him. His eyes seemed out of focus, as if looking at something far off. "You know," he lowered the gun, "you're right. Why don't we just clean this whole mess up now? You'll see that we had nothing to do with these murders. Oh sure, we took the bonds out, but there's absolutely nothing illegal about that. Let me just get a few papers I think I'll need to show the police."

"Okay," Lowell looked at his watch, "but don't take too long."

"I'll just be a minute." He opened the door to his inner office and turned. "Johnny," he said to Wally's manager, "give me a hand with these papers, will ya?"

"Sure, Larry." Gleason got up, followed him into the office, and closed the door.

"I swear Gene's death was an accident," said Frey. "The other two I don't know anything about."

"Well, it's really not my concern. I'm just going to give you all over to the cops and you can tell them your story." He looked at his watch. "Hey," he shouted, "hurry up in there."

"What's the rush?" asked Vivian, wiping her eyes.

"I had Andy call Lieutenant Roland and in about two minutes the police are going to come through that door, followed closely by the press. I would just as soon not be here when the reporters arrive." He got up, walked to the office door and knocked. Then he opened it. It was empty. "God damn it."

"What wrong?" asked Vivian.

"They're gone."

She looked in the office. "How, there's no other door?"

Lowell walked into the office followed by Vivian and began feeling along the walls. Then he went to Latner's desk and started handling the edges.

There was a loud pounding at the front door. "Vivian, would you?" She walked to the front door and opened it. Lieutenant Roland was the first one in.

Vivian pointed to the inner office. "I think you'd better talk to David."

Roland entered followed by two uniforms. "All right, Lowell, so where are your killers?"

"This is Richard Frey, Gene's manager. He'll tell you his side of things."

"Did he kill Freddie?"

"No," cried Frey, "I swear to Christ I never killed anybody. You got to believe me, Gene's death was an accident, an accident!"

"The other two came into this office and disappeared," said Lowell.

"What?" said Roland, "how?"

"I don't know yet, but I have a feeling…" Lowell was still fondling the desk when he heard a sharp clicking sound, and a wood panel that covered one wall of the office slid to the right revealing a passageway. "What is this? How terrific."

"What the hell?" asked Roland. "Who has secret passages in New York?"

"This is an old house," said Vivian. "Larry was very proud of it, said it was one of the first built up here about the turn of the last century. This was all wilderness and farms until about 1900."

"This must have originally been a connection to another building, maybe a barn," said Lowell.

They went through a short passageway and came to a door that led out onto the street via a basement exit.

"Well," said Roland, when they were standing on the sidewalk, "they must've hidden here till we came in and now they're long gone." He turned to one of the policemen. "Put out an APB." He turned to Lowell. "What are their names?"

"Larry Latner and Johnny Gleason. I'll give your men a description."

They went back through the tunnel and into the office.

"I'm going to need statements from you two."

"Lieutenant, I think it would be prudent for me to get Ms. Younger out of here as soon as possible. The press should be along anytime. We can meet you at your office and straighten this out later."

"Agreed. Go."

Lowell took Vivian by the arm and hurried out the front door only to be confronted by a wall of reporters and photographers already interviewing the cops at the scene.

"Vivian," one shouted, "over here."

He took their picture. Then a barrage of cameras exploded in their faces. One of the reporters recognized Lowell and stuck a microphone in front of him. "Mr. Lowell, were you involved in this case?"

"Only peripherally. It was solved by Lieutenant Roland of the NYPD. I only had a small hand in aiding the police in this matter."

"That's not what my sources tell me. I have it on excellent authority that you cracked this case and led the police here to the office of Freddie Finger's manager, Larry Latner."

"No comment."

"Vivian, what do you think about this? Was it really your father's manager that killed him? And why?"

Lowell put his arm around Vivian, waved the reporter away, and pushed through the crowd. Andy was waiting at the corner. They jumped into the back seat and sped away.

Chapter Forty

The next day Lowell and Vivian were at the precinct.

As they came into his office Roland held up a copy of the *New York Post*.

"Did you see this?"

"Yes," said Lowell, "I saw it."

"*Astrologer Solves Rock 'n Roll Murders*. You did get to see the whole story, didn't you? If not, I would be happy to read how you single-handedly figured out who the murderer was and lead the inept New York City police right to his door."

"Lieutenant, I…"

Roland held up his hand. "Here's one line I particularly like: *When asked about his role in the case the modest Mr. Lowell replied, 'I only had a small hand in aiding the police in this matter.'* The modest Mr. Lowell."

"But Lieutenant," interjected Vivian, "that *is* what he said. You can't believe that David purposely took the credit."

"Heaven forbid."

"At least he solved my father's murder." She was going to add that she doubted the police would have been able to, but she caught Lowell looking at her, faintly shaking his head, and stopped.

"I do owe you that," said Roland. "But you should have called us before you went to Latner's house. Then at least maybe he and Gleason wouldn't have gotten away."

"You still don't have them?" asked Lowell.

"No."

"They're heading for the Cayman Islands. That's where the cash is. Neptune is most prominent in his chart right now."

Roland frowned. "Whatever the hell that means."

"That means watch the waterways. He's going to try to get there by boat, not plane. And don't worry, you'll get him. With Pluto about to afflict the ruler of Latner's 12th house his chart shows a long incarceration."

"Well, at least we finally know who did it," said Roland.

"What did you get from Frey?"

"He swears Gene's death was an accident. It's going to be hard to get him for that one, as there were no witnesses, no evidence at all. Who know, maybe he's telling the truth. He also denies knowing anything about Wally's or Freddie's murders. He does admit to being part of the bond deal, although he says he doesn't know anything about the murders or the Cayman Islands."

Lowell and Vivian gave extensive interviews to the police. When they were finished he took her back to her hotel.

"I'm so tired," she said. "Can we get together later?"

"Of course. This has been an exacting time for you."

He left her and went back to the office.

Boredom is the worst thing for a thinking person. If Lowell had only a dollar and an impending train ride, he would spend it on a newspaper rather than food, no matter how hungry or thirsty he might be.

He looked at the messages Sarah had left for him. There were a few astrology clients he needed to call back, but the rest was just nonsense, reporters, TV shows, magazines looking for sensational interviews. There was one offer from the Food Network that made him laugh out loud. Could he possibly join Emeril Lagassi in a show about cooking for the different astrology signs?

How, he wondered, *did we manage to invent an entire culture without substance?*

Chapter Forty-one

Marty clutched the bag as he slowly walked up the stairs to his apartment. He hated to admit it but he was finally feeling his age. This had been a draining experience. He was tired, tired of it all.

New York, his home for so many years, was feeling like a washed-up relationship, clinging to the memories of passion when none is left. The sparkle dulled and the gallant struggle turned to rage and frustration.

Maybe he would go to Nashville. At least he knew some people there. Everyone he knew in New York was either dead or out of work and wished they were dead.

He opened the door to his apartment.

"Hi." Beth was sitting on the futon watching the tiny TV. She looked very cute clad only in his partly closed bathrobe with her long, black, wet hair hanging down over her eyes.

Marty smiled. "You're home early."

"I had enough of my sister and her kids. Four weeks as Aunt Beth is plenty, believe me. I hope you don't mind that I came over to shower. I missed you."

"I'm glad to see you." He leaned over and gave her a strong kiss.

"How have things been? I feel like I haven't spoken to you in ages. It was tough to get cell phone reception on the Cape."

"I know, it's okay."

"You look tired. Want to talk about it?"

He put the bag on the table. It landed with a 'clunk.'

"What's that?" asked Beth.

"A piece of my past. Take a look."

She reached into the bag and took out a heavy coin. "What is this?"

"What's it look like?"

"Gold."

"Bingo."

She poured the contents of the bag onto the table. "How many are there?"

"Thirty three."

"What are they worth?"

"Seventeen hundred each, give or take."

"Wow. That's a lot."

"About fifty six thousand dollars." He laughed. "It used to be a lot of money, but it won't last as long these days. Still…"

"Is it yours?"

"Yep."

"What are you going to do with it?"

"I don't know."

"So where did this come from?"

"It's a long story."

"I've got plenty of time." She opened the drawer and took out the pot, filled a pipe and handed it to Marty. "Here, you take the first hit."

He smoked and then gave it to her. Then he told her all about Freddie and the gold, Lowell and the cops.

When he finished she was too stunned to speak for a moment. "I never knew you knew Freddie Finger that well."

He nodded. "Since we were kids. I knew a bunch of the stars back in the eighties. But what's the difference now?"

"Have you thought about what we discussed?"

"Of course I have."

"Well, what do you think?"

"Do you really want to live together?"

She was forty-three, he was fifty-nine. If he could provide some security he would jump at the chance to spend his years with her. She was funny and smart, had a good political sensitivity and she really liked his music. But all of his past relationships had failed for the same reason, no money.

"You know what you're in store for, don't you? I've never made much of a living, so I doubt that we're in for wonderful surprises and trips to the Riviera."

She smiled.

"And if you think that I'm easy to deal with on a daily basis, then you're in for a terrible shock."

"Anything else?"

"Not that I can think of right now."

She got up and went to the refrigerator, took out a bottle of grape juice and poured a glass. She put the bottle back in the fridge. "We would have one rent, which we could split. I make a pretty good living. Besides, you don't look your age."

"For how long?"

"Well," she smirked, "when you start looking old I'll just leave you out in the woods." She sat on his lap and held up one of the coins. "At least we don't have to worry for a little while. We could consider this an omen, a chance for a new life, maybe use it as a down payment on a small home like we've always talked about. What do you say?"

"If you don't mind taking a chance on an old man."

"So I can take that as a yes?"

"I guess so."

She leaped on top of him pushing him down on the futon and kissed him.

The phone rang.

"Leave it," she said.

"No, I've got to. Things have been so weird lately."

He picked up the phone. "Hello?"

"Hello," said the voice on the other end. "Is this Marty Winebeck?"

"Yes."

"This is Gloria Goodman from the New York Theatrical Organization."

"What can I do for you?"

"We were given a copy of your play and music and we'd like to discuss development of the property."

"Do you mind telling me how you heard about me?"

"It was sent to us anonymously. We're all very excited about the project, and anxious to get together with you to discuss it."

If this was a scam to get a few bucks from him he wasn't about to fall for it. It was better to get the phonies out of the way right at the beginning. "But, I'm an unknown playwright. Why would you want to take a chance on my work?"

"Well, for one thing," said Ms. Goodman, "we are very impressed with your project, especially the music. The general consensus is that your melodies and lyrics are extremely fresh and exciting, and that with a little shaking, your book can support your wonderful score."

"And, just how much is this going to cost me?"

"Cost *you*? Not a cent. Your job is to get the play and score into shape, that's all. You see, the book and CD also came with a letter promising a one hundred thousand dollar check to help cover the costs of a production, if we all agree on the project."

"A hundred thousand dollars?"

"It's not as unusual as you may think for patrons to approach small not-for-profit theatre groups and offer to help their friends. It gets their play to the public, and helps us remain in business. You must have some very loyal fans willing to put their money where their mouth is."

"I don't know what to say."

"We want you to know that even with the generous donation of your supporters, if we didn't believe in the project we wouldn't waste our time or yours producing it. We only put on six productions a year and each one must be up to our standards. The money is incidental, although the offer did get our attention."

After taking their address and promising to come by the next day he hung up and repeated the conversation verbatim to Beth.

"Who do you think it was?" asked Beth.

"I think that the answer is in the stars."

"What do you want to do to celebrate? Let's go somewhere and try to pay the bill with one of these." She held up a coin.

"I know where we should go."

"Where?"

"B. B. King's."

She was surprised. Marty didn't like going out to live shows.

"Really? Who's playing there?"

"Me."

Chapter Forty-two

The Ivy League Club is an impressive looking building on West 43rd Street. As Lowell turned the corner he spied Vivian talking with another woman and approached.

"Hi," he said," glad you could make it."

Vivian kissed him briefly on the lips. "This is my friend Ellen."

"How do you do," he turned toward the brunette.

"Nice to finally meet you," said Ellen. "I've heard so much about you from Vivian. I'm really looking forward to your lecture."

"Thank you," Lowell was taken aback. It never occurred to him that Vivian would talk about him to her friends, and certainly not to the point of *I've heard so much about you.* "I've seen you somewhere, haven't I?"

"Ellen is the star of *Found*, the number one TV show in America."

"That's right. You're wonderful, I've enjoyed your work immensely."

"Thank you. That's so nice to hear."

He almost never watched commercial TV and had never seen the show. He must have seen her face in a passing promo and it stuck in his memory.

They entered the club and took the elevator to the fourth floor. The hallway was crowded with about twenty people milling around, some holding red wine in plastic cups.

Lowell spied his host, Ed Sutter, and walked over.

"Nice crowd tonight," said the astrologer.

"It seems your notoriety precedes you. They've given you the James Madison Room. It's the biggest one we have."

◇◇◇

After the lecture Lowell met Vivian and Ellen and together they escaped the crowd.

"That was wonderful," said Ellen. "I had no idea astrology was such a fascinating subject. And you really predicted all those things including nine-eleven and the stock market crash?"

"Unfortunately, yes."

"Why unfortunately?"

"It only showed me how impotent individuals are to change things."

"You tried to warn people?" asked Ellen.

"I did little to hide my views. I have published a monthly astrology newsletter since 1999 and continued to predict the effects of Saturn in opposition to Pluto in the sky in 2001 on top of America's ascendant. I was on national radio, TV, and in print anywhere I could. I wasn't alone. Several other astrologers had come to the same conclusion, to no avail."

Vivian smiled. "I think your work is very important and will eventually have a great impact."

"Perhaps, if I live long enough. The older you get the more respect you can demand in astrological circles."

Both actresses laughed.

"You don't know how lucky you are," said Vivian.

"Yeah," Ellen nodded her head, "in our business it's just the opposite. You reach that age of undesirability and then have to find something useful to do with the rest of your life."

"That's too bad. I find that it takes a lifetime to perfect any skill. My guess is that most actors are better when they are older."

"That's probably true," said Ellen, "if they could find the roles suitable to prove it." She looked at her cell phone. "Oh my, I had no idea it was so late. This has been great fun, but I have to run."

"Can't you join us for a drink?" asked Vivian.

"I'd love to, but I've got an early shoot tomorrow. We're filming in New York all week. Besides," she smiled at Lowell, "I think you've got enough company."

◇◇◇

Lowell and Vivian went to Rue 57 on 57th Street and Sixth Avenue and sat at a small table near the bar. A few people recognized Vivian but didn't approach her.

She had a Lillet on the rocks with a slice of orange. Lowell had a Beck's.

When the drinks arrived he took her hand. "You seem a little distant."

"I'm sorry, David, this has all been too much for me, I'm afraid."

"I know it must have been hell since he died."

"Thank god for you."

He squeezed her hand.

She gently took her hand back and picked up her drink. "I was blind. I knew what people said about my father but I only believed what I wanted to. I never realized how much he hurt people. Larry Latner was family. He would send me gifts on Christmas and my birthday, even before my mother let me see my father. Later he took me ice skating and to museums and came over for holidays. My father looked up to him. I looked up to him." She sipped her drink. "And I looked up to my father."

"And they all let you down in the end."

"Maybe it's time for me to stop looking for a father figure to lean on and learn to rely on myself.

Lowell felt the pang of imminent loss. She was right, of course. But that was what he had become, another father figure. And as often happened in his profession when he became close to a client, he still had to advise them to do what was best for them, even if it wasn't always best for him.

"I need to be alone for a while," she said.

"I understand."

"I'm going back to LA tomorrow and think through some of this. I may begin therapy again, I don't know."

Lowell nodded.

"Will you come and visit me?"

"If you like."

She turned toward him. "Yes, I think I would."

"You'll let me know."

"I'm sorry this happened when it did. You never let me down. Now I feel as though I'm letting you down."

"I'm just glad for the short time we had. I'll cherish it."

"Can we please talk on the phone soon? Maybe when I've had a few months to sort through all of this…"

"Maybe."

Chapter Forty-three

Lowell was tired. It always happened after a case, but this one had been so physically and emotionally exhilarating that the letdown was particularly noticeable.

Sarah buzzed.

He picked up the phone.

"Your buddies are back."

The door opened and the three rockers entered.

"Hey," said Bobby, "nice job."

"Yeah," said Pete, "I can't believe it was their managers."

"I can," said Barron.

"I always told you they were trouble," said Bobby.

"Well," replied Pete, "you should know. You had more than your share of problems with them."

"How did you know?" asked Barron.

"Astrology."

The others nodded, respect showed on their faces.

"So what now?" asked Lowell.

"For us?" asked Pete.

"Yeah."

"We'll just keep on touring and recording."

"Why would you want to bust your hump at your age? I can't believe any of you need the money."

Barron answered. "You know why we make so much money touring?"

"I assume it's because everybody loves your work and probably wants to see you before you retire."

"Maybe. But I like to think it's because they all want to be at that concert when one of us croaks. Can you imagine how much those tickets would sell for on EBay?" He laughed heartily.

"So if it's not about the money, and it's not about the girls anymore, what's it all for?"

Barron shrugged. "It's about the music, just like it always was."

"We've all got a job to do," said Pete. "And we've got to keep doing it."

There was more to it, and Lowell knew it. Remaining relevant in a changing world. But he said nothing.

"If you ever want to see a show let us know," said Barron. "You've got our cell phones. You never know, you might get lucky and hit the EBay jackpot."

"Hey," said Bobby on the way out, "let's have lunch."

◇◇◇

All Lowell wanted to do now was gather his things and head home. He required nothing more than a cool shower and a few days lounging around the townhouse in jeans and a t-shirt. He longed to sit in his backyard beneath the sycamore tree and read the *Times* at his leisure.

He spun his chair around, leaned back, and looked at the Empire State Building glistening in the distance.

Sarah came in carrying a checkbook. "What do you want me to do with the check from Vivian Younger?"

He turned the chair around to face her. "The same as always."

She nodded. "I assumed as much."

She ripped out a check, which had no name or address printed on it, and wrote it for the exact amount as the fee, made it out to the police retirement fund, and sent it off anonymously.

"I read *Shibumi*," she said.

"You did?"

"What a sad story."

"Women only see the emotional side of the parable."

"Got any other books you would recommend?"

"Sure, I'd love to make out a reading list for you."

"It's a sad business."

"What, the music business?"

"The human business. What do you think it is, a comedy or a tragedy?"

"It's both at the same time. It's up to us which way we want to view it."

"Anything can be funny?"

"Well, maybe not funny exactly, but used to your advantage."

"Like the fruit?"

He nodded. "If you break your leg in early July you can bitch and moan about how much summer fun you're missing or you can try to write a novel. Either way your leg will still be in that cast."

"Pollyanna," replied the red head.

"No, I'm too realistic to be called that."

"What then?"

"A seeker."

"Of what?"

"Shibumi."

She thought about that for a moment, and then nodded. "Look, if you need me you've got my cell phone. But do me a favor and don't need me for a few days. I'm going to be with Philip."

"Philip?"

"Vivian's chauffeur," she giggled. "You knew, didn't you?"

"I knew there was a good chance someone new would be coming along and I figured it would look a lot better than your worn out relationship with Rudy."

"Well, you were right again."

"It was your free will that made it happen, always remember that."

She picked up her purse and was about to leave. She hesitated.

"I just wanted to say," she stopped to gather her thoughts. "I just wanted to say that this is fun, all of it, even the scary parts.

I would have been stuck working as a social worker and fighting for my life on the subway every morning. I could never ask for a better job. Thank you."

She kissed him on the cheek and started to leave.

"You're welcome. Oh, and Sarah…"

She turned back.

"Would you please take these flowers out of here?"

Chapter Forty-four

The heat finally broke on Friday. Lowell was in the office in the basement of his townhouse finishing the report on the case.

They had found Latner and Gleason off the coast of Key West in a small fishing boat heading to the Caymans, as Lowell had predicted. Roland was able to gather enough physical evidence for an indictment and a conviction was virtually guaranteed. He didn't envy them. Freddie and Wally had a lot of fans, some of whom were likely incarcerated and might like a chance to express their disappointment directly toward the two.

His encounter with Vivian had awakened long dormant feelings he thought were gone forever. How can such a short interlude alter our perception so much?

He sipped his herbal tea.

Since Robert's death he had hardened his shell, rarely allowing his feelings free reign. How could he? But now a single unguarded moment of passion had stripped away the façade those walls conveyed, exposing them as the fog they really were, more Neptune than Saturn, more illusion than reality.

Three times he picked up the phone and three times he put it back down. He walked over to the window and looked out at his tiny empire, gazing at the flowers so gently cared for by Julia. He sighed. It had been so long since he had experienced any real emotions he wasn't quite sure how to process the information.

He felt about sixteen, just the way he had felt right after his first intimate encounter with a woman. He was amazed, and scared, and just a little ashamed all at the same time.

But mostly he felt alive. Vivian had awakened a primal need for companionship that had been denied since his divorce. *"The man is nothing, the work is all,"* he was fond of saying. But in some ways maybe that philosophy had come to serve as an excuse not to open up to another person. Vivian took control and he had followed. He never could have taken the initiative at this age. He owed her more than he could ever repay, the breath of life pushed into a dying soul. To live without connection isn't to live at all. But we can't always see it.

In many ways she reminded him of his ex-wife, Catherine, when they first got together: young, beautiful, vivacious, and so very vulnerable. As the years progressed Catherine became stronger and less reliant on his guiding hand. But never less beautiful. They had been drifting apart for some time before Robert's death. That was just the final push. After all this time he still didn't know why. But he did know that his defenses had kicked in and he didn't know how to stop them.

His Sun fell on Catherine's Moon. That in itself is often enough reason for a marriage. But they had so many planetary connections it would take a two hour lecture to explain it all. And yet, all of that couldn't keep the marriage going once the egos got in the way.

What motivated people to do what Latner had done? What was the real underlying drive? He had been a wealthy man, before all of this nonsense about the bonds. He didn't really need the money, so why go so such extremes to get more? And once his scheme failed, was it really worth the weight on his mortal soul to commit murder?

Or was there more to it? Was Freud right and everything was about sex?

Perhaps Latner had defended his family the only way he could. But was it about his daughter, or the years he put up with Freddie screwing his wife? And in the long run, did it matter?

He pushed the tea away, opened the small refrigerator by his desk and took out a Spatan beer and a chilled mug. He opened the bottle and poured the contents into the icy glass, then took a sip. He loved a quote attributed to Ben Franklin: *Beer is proof that god loves us.*

Latner and Gleason would most likely spend the rest of their lives in prison. The financial repercussions would be felt for years to come, and the already struggling recording industry was being attacked by Internet music companies who used the murders as further proof that artists didn't need the establishment of the old record industry to create and reach a public. Latner had done even more damage to the business he loved so much.

He took a sip of his beer, sat on the small couch, and picked up the phone again. He couldn't believe how much he missed her. How he yearned just to hear the sound of her voice. This time he dialed the number and listened as it connected. It rang three times with no response. On the fourth ring he was about to hang up when she answered.

"Hello?"

He didn't know what to say, what he even wanted. He took a deep breath.

"Hello."

"David?"

"Yes."

"How are you? Is everything alright?"

"Hello, Catherine, I was just...thinking about you."

To receive a free catalog of Poisoned Pen Press titles, please contact us in one of the following ways:

Phone: 1-800-421-3976
Facsimile: 1-480-949-1707
Email: info@poisonedpenpress.com
Website: www.poisonedpenpress.com

Poisoned Pen Press
6962 E. First Ave. Ste 103
Scottsdale, AZ 85251